D0399940

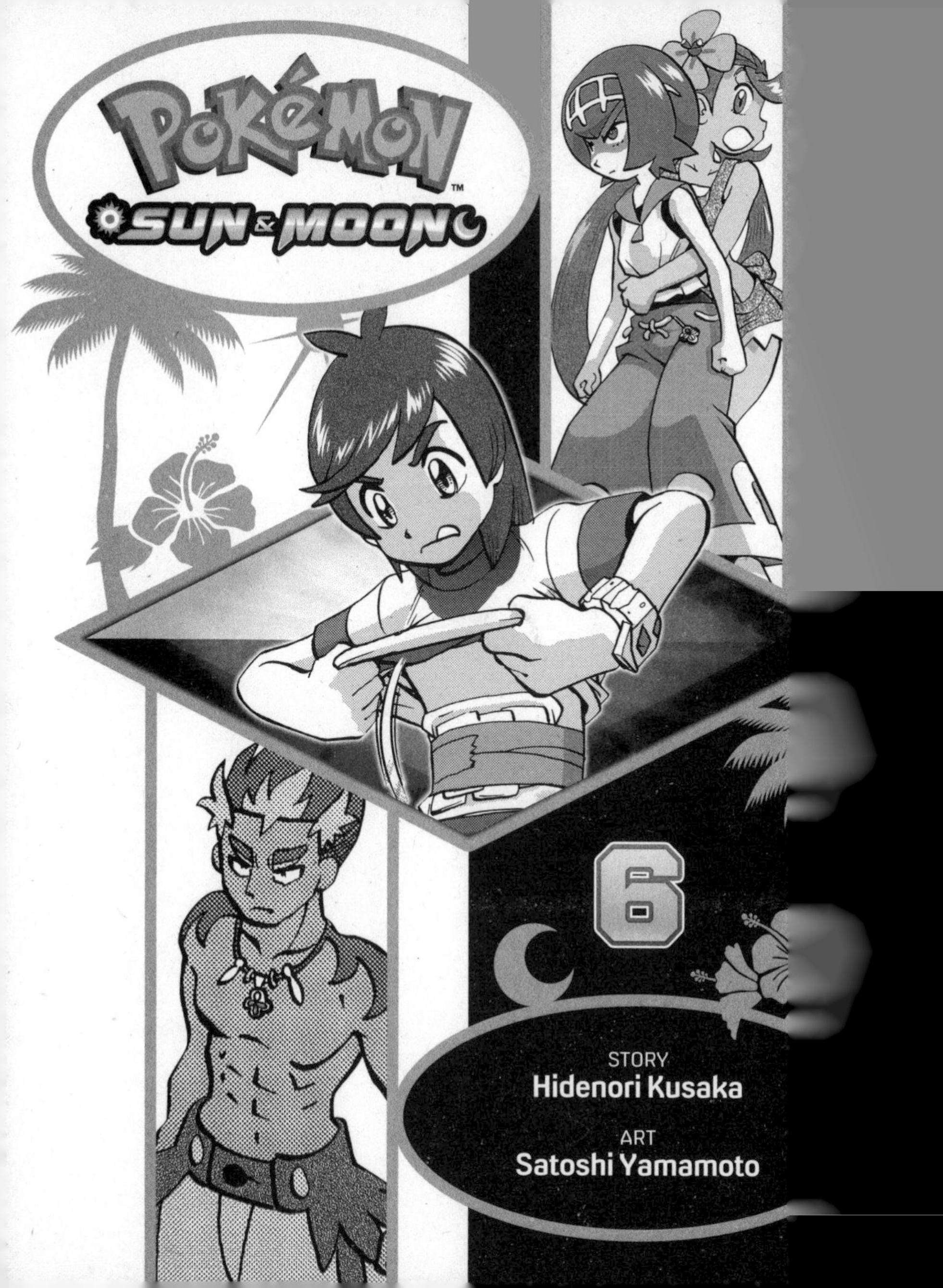
POKÉMON™
SUN & MOON
6
STORY
Hidenori Kusaka
ART
Satoshi Yamamoto

Introduction

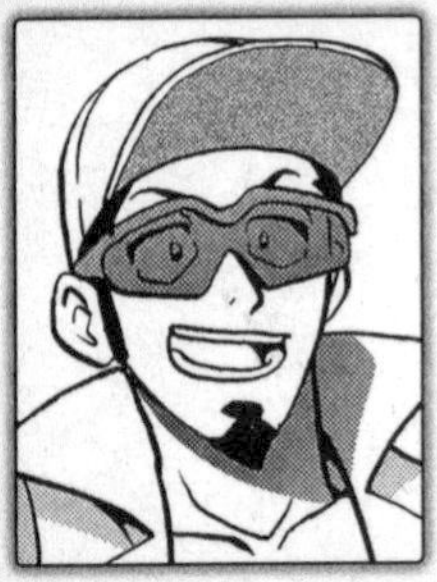

Professor Kukui

A Pokémon researcher with a laboratory on Melemele Island. An expert on Pokémon moves who likes to experience these Pokémon moves used against himself!

Moon

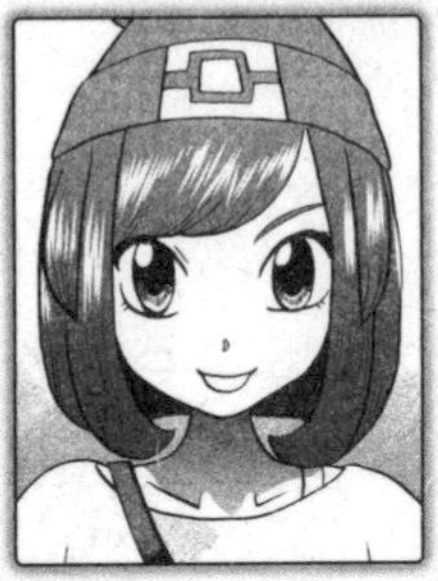

Another of the main characters of this tale. A pharmacist who has traveled to Alola from a faraway region. She is a self-confident, original thinker. She is also an excellent archer.

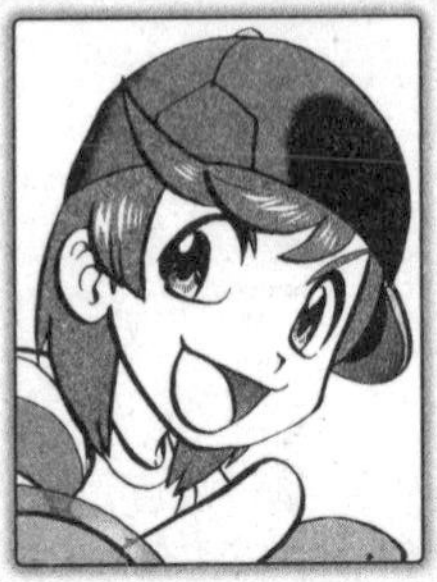

Sun

One of the main characters of this tale. A young Pokémon Trainer who makes a living doing all sorts of odd jobs, including working as a delivery boy. His dream is to save up a million dollars!

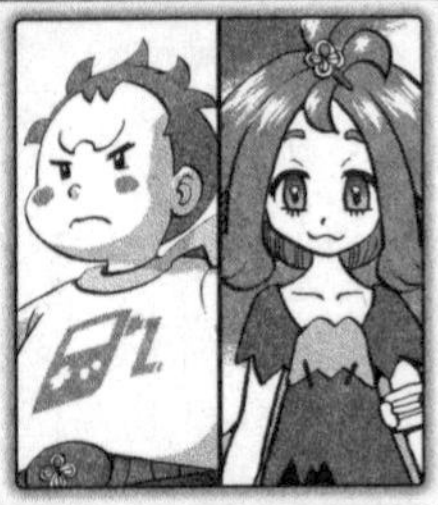

Acerola/ Sophocles

Skilled Trainers and the trial captains of Ula'ula Island.

Kiawe, Mallow, Lana

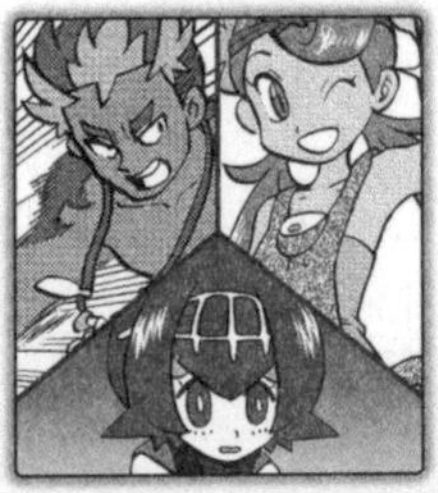

Skilled Trainers and the trial captains of Akala Island.

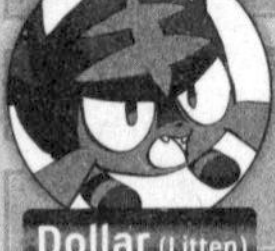

Dollar (Litten)

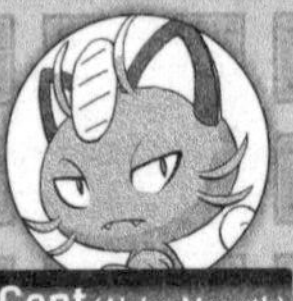

Cent (Alolan Meowth)

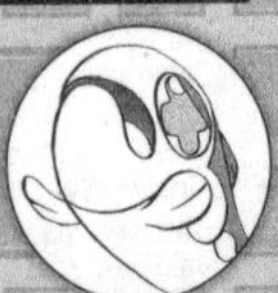

Quarter (Wishiwashi)

Character

Guzma

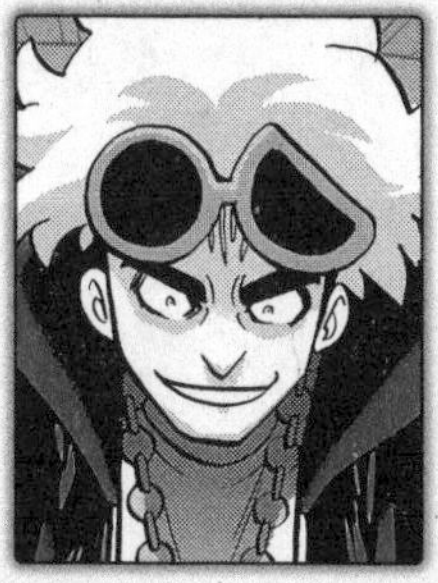

The leader of Team Skull, an evil organization that is causing trouble all over the Alola region.

Lillie

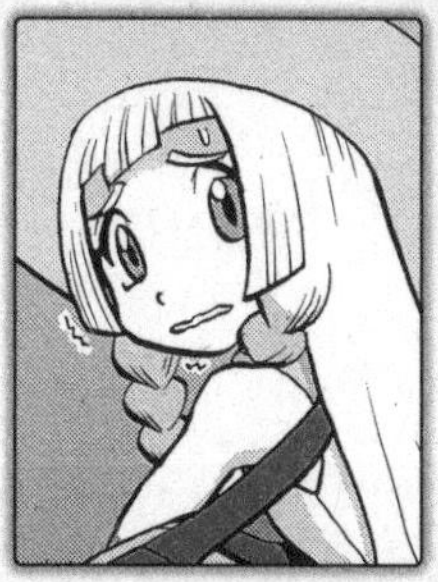

A timid girl found washed up on the beach. She carries a strange Pokémon whom she calls Nebby.

Gladion

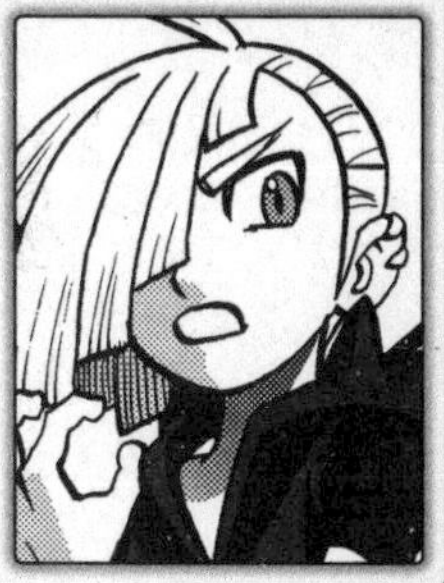

A loner with a mysterious Pokémon named Type: Null. Why is he so interested in a mysterious rift in the sky...?

The Story Thus Far...

The Alola region consists of numerous tropical islands. Moon, a pharmacist from another region, comes to this flower-filled vacation paradise on an important errand. On one of Alola's pristine beaches, she meets a boy named Sun. Sun works various odd jobs in addition to the delivery service he runs in order to reach his goal of saving up a million dollars. Moon doesn't understand why he would want so much money, but they become friends and travel to Professor Kukui's laboratory together. Meanwhile, at Iki Town on Melemele Island, preparations are in full swing for the Full Power Festival...

Each of the four islands of Alola have an Island Guardian called a Tapu. Recently, the Tapu have become agitated... The island leaders use the festival's Pokémon tournament to choose a champion to get to the root of the problem and soothe the Tapu. So when Sun defeats Gladion in the final match, he is sent off on the Island Challenge with Moon. On Akala Island, Moon witnesses a battle between Tapu Lele and a mysterious being who appears through a rift in the sky. Sun wins the respect of the Alola trial captains in battle and then fights Gladion again—this time for real—at the Ruins of Life. Sun defeats him by using the Z-Move that Kiawe taught him. Then, while the trial captains search for the headquarters of Team Skull, Sun embarks on Acerola's next trial...

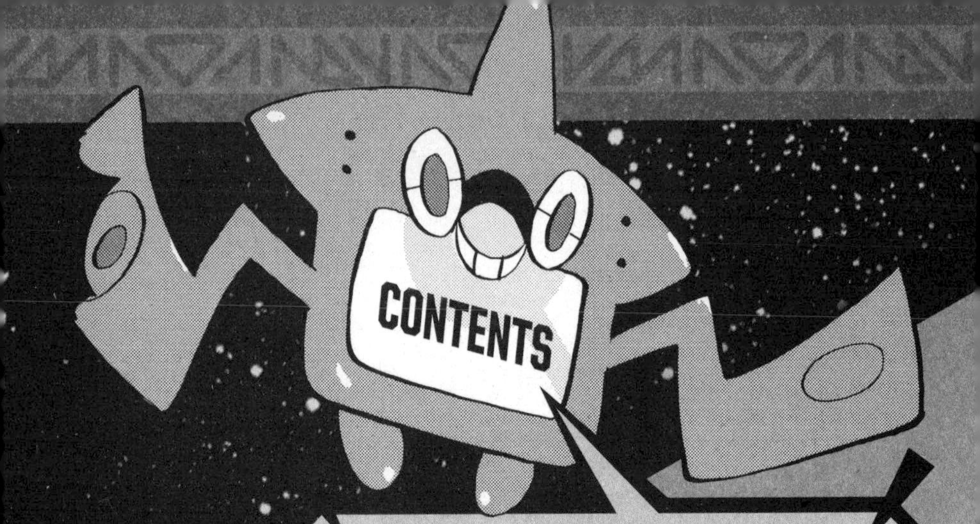

CONTENTS

Zzt zzt...♫

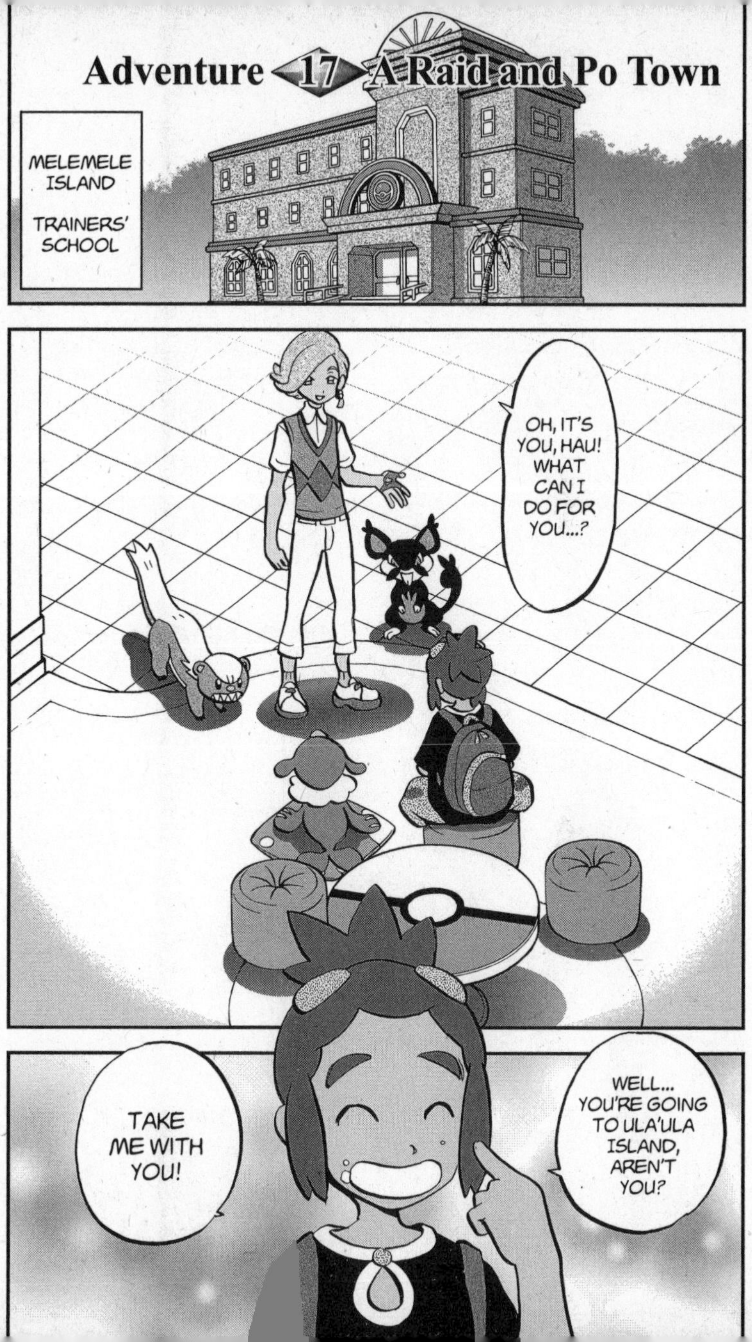
Adventure 17 A Raid and Po Town
MELEMELE ISLAND
TRAINERS' SCHOOL
OH, IT'S YOU, HAU! WHAT CAN I DO FOR YOU...?
WELL... YOU'RE GOING TO ULA'ULA ISLAND, AREN'T YOU?
TAKE ME WITH YOU!

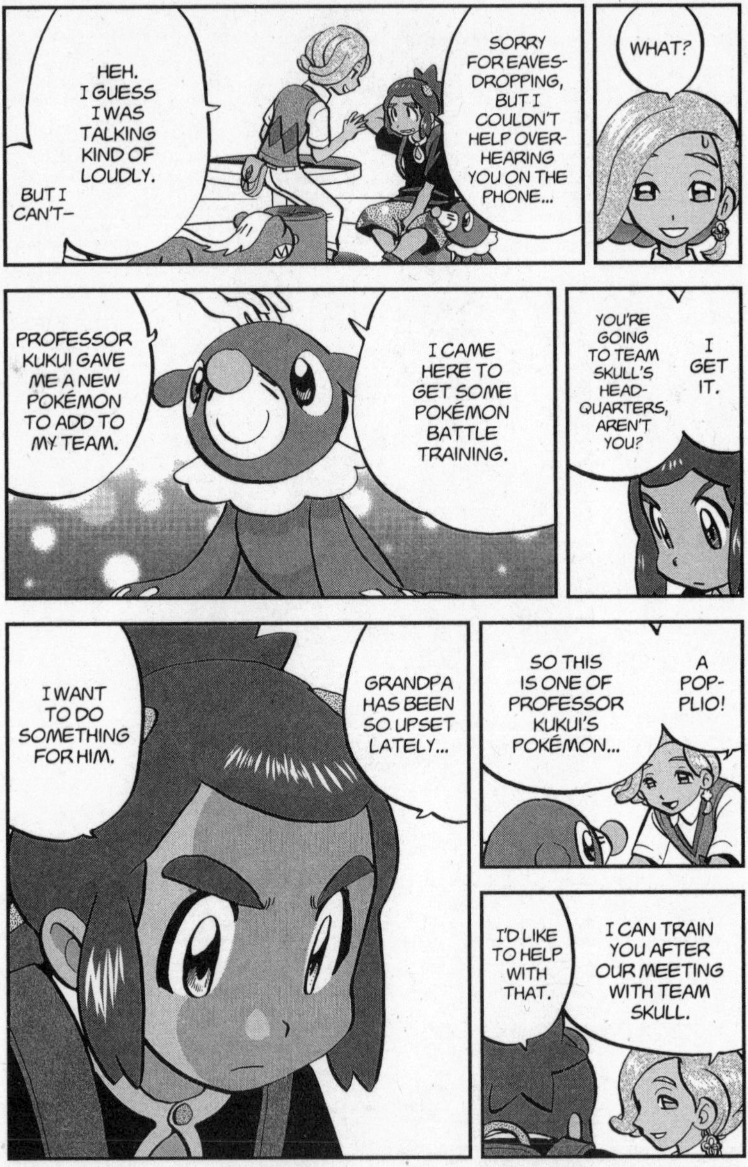
WHAT?
SORRY FOR EAVES-DROPPING, BUT I COULDN'T HELP OVER-HEARING YOU ON THE PHONE...
HEH. I GUESS I WAS TALKING KIND OF LOUDLY.
BUT I CAN'T-
I GET IT.
YOU'RE GOING TO TEAM SKULL'S HEAD-QUARTERS, AREN'T YOU?
I CAME HERE TO GET SOME POKÉMON BATTLE TRAINING.
PROFESSOR KUKUI GAVE ME A NEW POKÉMON TO ADD TO MY TEAM.
A POP-PLIO!
SO THIS IS ONE OF PROFESSOR KUKUI'S POKÉMON...
I CAN TRAIN YOU AFTER OUR MEETING WITH TEAM SKULL.
I'D LIKE TO HELP WITH THAT.
GRANDPA HAS BEEN SO UPSET LATELY...
I WANT TO DO SOMETHING FOR HIM.

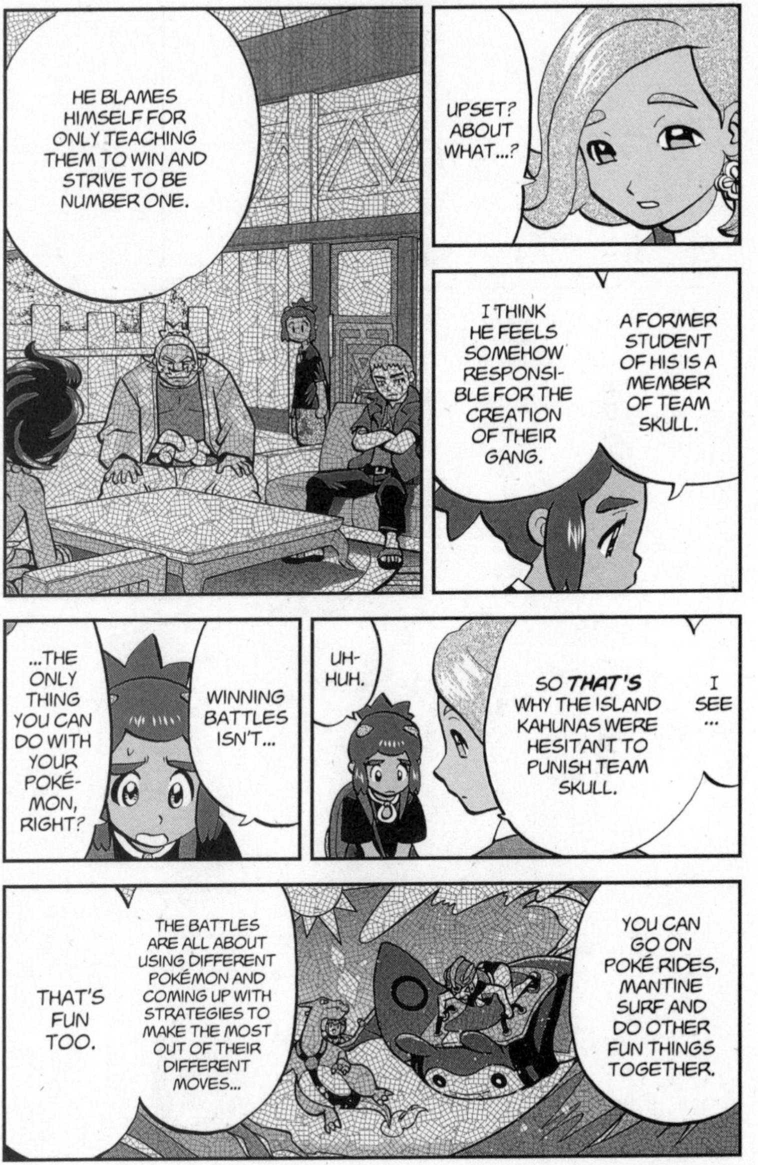
UPSET? ABOUT WHAT...?
A FORMER STUDENT OF HIS IS A MEMBER OF TEAM SKULL.
I THINK HE FEELS SOMEHOW RESPONSIBLE FOR THE CREATION OF THEIR GANG.
HE BLAMES HIMSELF FOR ONLY TEACHING THEM TO WIN AND STRIVE TO BE NUMBER ONE.
I SEE...
SO ***THAT'S*** WHY THE ISLAND KAHUNAS WERE HESITANT TO PUNISH TEAM SKULL.
UH-HUH.
WINNING BATTLES ISN'T...
...THE ONLY THING YOU CAN DO WITH YOUR POKÉMON, RIGHT?
YOU CAN GO ON POKÉ RIDES, MANTINE SURF AND DO OTHER FUN THINGS TOGETHER.
THE BATTLES ARE ALL ABOUT USING DIFFERENT POKÉMON AND COMING UP WITH STRATEGIES TO MAKE THE MOST OUT OF THEIR DIFFERENT MOVES...
THAT'S FUN TOO.

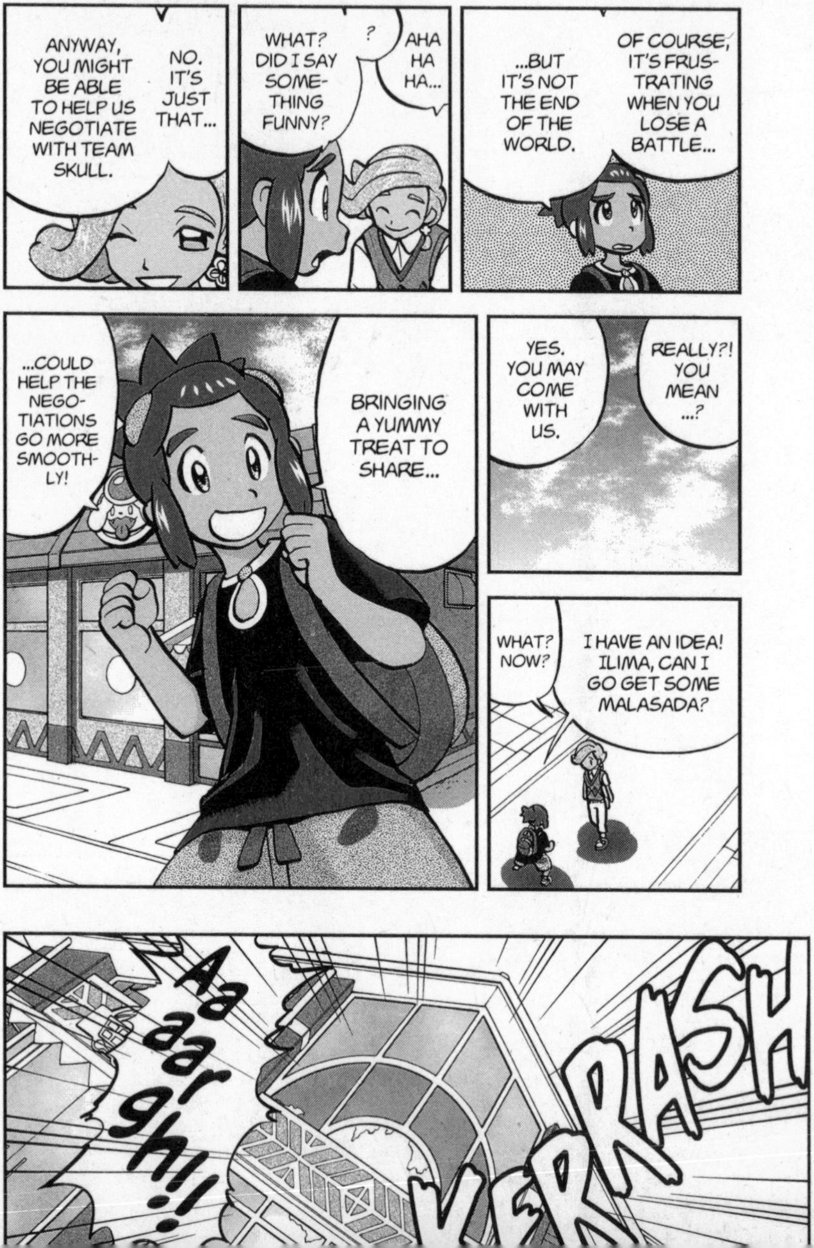
OF COURSE, IT'S FRUS-TRATING WHEN YOU LOSE A BATTLE...
...BUT IT'S NOT THE END OF THE WORLD.
AHA HA HA...
?
WHAT? DID I SAY SOME-THING FUNNY?
NO. IT'S JUST THAT...
ANYWAY, YOU MIGHT BE ABLE TO HELP US NEGOTIATE WITH TEAM SKULL.
REALLY?! YOU MEAN ...?
YES. YOU MAY COME WITH US.
I HAVE AN IDEA! ILIMA, CAN I GO GET SOME MALASADA?
WHAT? NOW?
BRINGING A YUMMY TREAT TO SHARE...
...COULD HELP THE NEGO-TIATIONS GO MORE SMOOTH-LY!
KERRASH
Aaaarrgh!!!

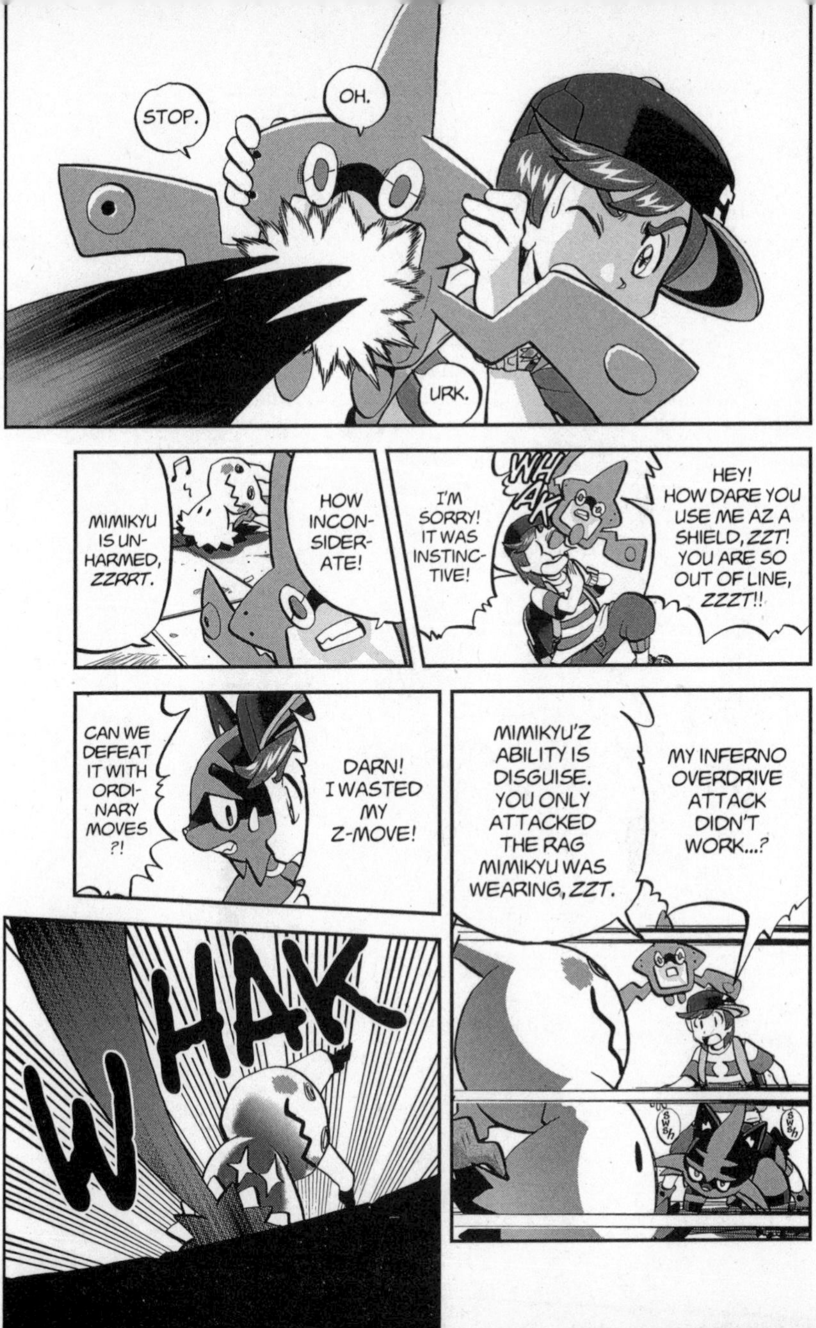
OH.
STOP.
URK.
WHAK
HEY! HOW DARE YOU USE ME AZ A SHIELD, ZZT! YOU ARE SO OUT OF LINE, ZZZT!!
I'M SORRY! IT WAS INSTINCTIVE!
HOW INCONSIDERATE!
MIMIKYU IS UNHARMED, ZZRRT.
MY INFERNO OVERDRIVE ATTACK DIDN'T WORK...?
MIMIKYU'Z ABILITY IS DISGUISE. YOU ONLY ATTACKED THE RAG MIMIKYU WAS WEARING, ZZT.
DARN! I WASTED MY Z-MOVE!
CAN WE DEFEAT IT WITH ORDINARY MOVES?!
SWISH
SWISH
WHAK

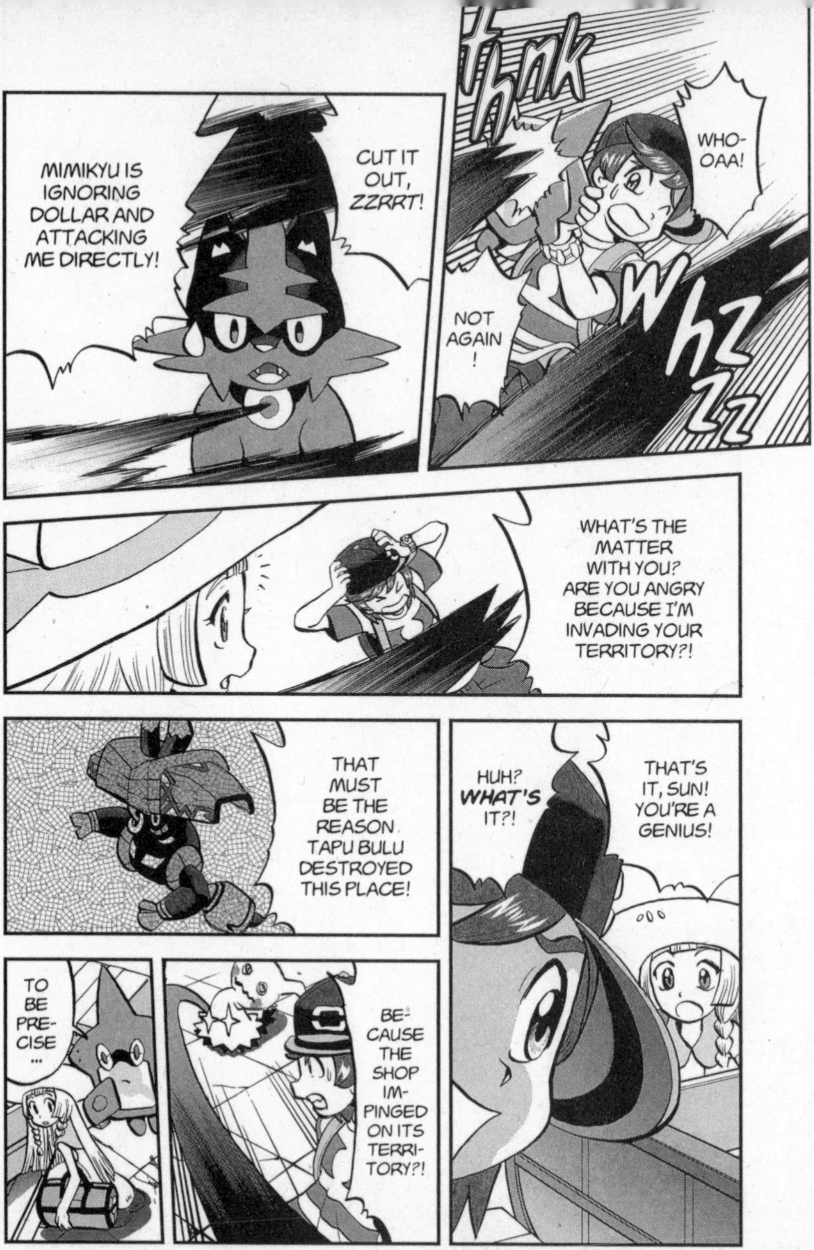
thnk
WHO-OAA!
NOT AGAIN!
Whzzz
CUT IT OUT, ZZRRT!
MIMIKYU IS IGNORING DOLLAR AND ATTACKING ME DIRECTLY!
WHAT'S THE MATTER WITH YOU? ARE YOU ANGRY BECAUSE I'M INVADING YOUR TERRITORY?!
THAT'S IT, SUN! YOU'RE A GENIUS!
HUH? **WHAT'S** IT?!
THAT MUST BE THE REASON TAPU BULU DESTROYED THIS PLACE!
BECAUSE THE SHOP IMPINGED ON ITS TERRITORY?!
TO BE PRECISE...

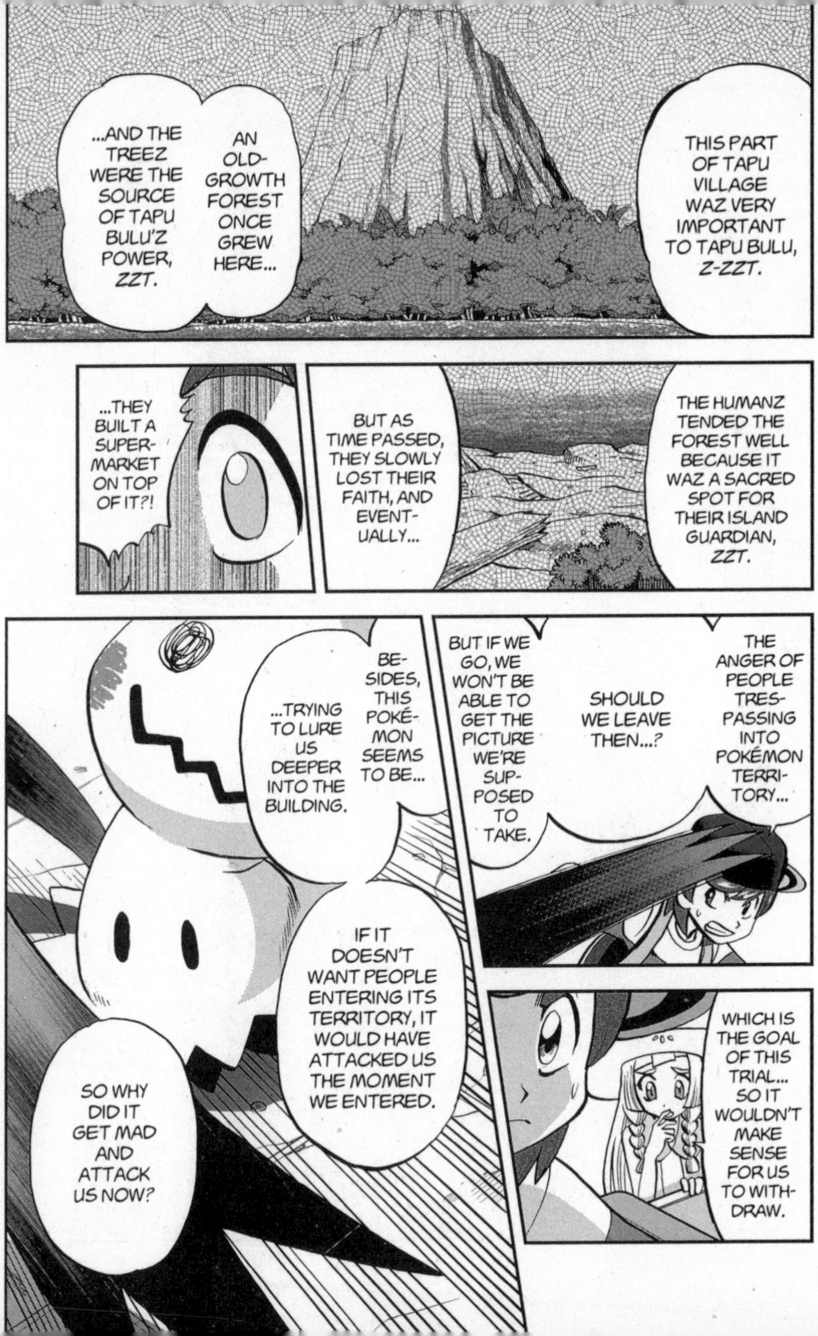
THIS PART OF TAPU VILLAGE WAZ VERY IMPORTANT TO TAPU BULU, Z-ZZT.
AN OLD-GROWTH FOREST ONCE GREW HERE...
...AND THE TREEZ WERE THE SOURCE OF TAPU BULU'Z POWER, ZZT.
THE HUMANZ TENDED THE FOREST WELL BECAUSE IT WAZ A SACRED SPOT FOR THEIR ISLAND GUARDIAN, ZZT.
BUT AS TIME PASSED, THEY SLOWLY LOST THEIR FAITH, AND EVENT-UALLY...
...THEY BUILT A SUPER-MARKET ON TOP OF IT?!
THE ANGER OF PEOPLE TRES-PASSING INTO POKÉMON TERRI-TORY...
SHOULD WE LEAVE THEN...?
BUT IF WE GO, WE WON'T BE ABLE TO GET THE PICTURE WE'RE SUP-POSED TO TAKE.
WHICH IS THE GOAL OF THIS TRIAL... SO IT WOULDN'T MAKE SENSE FOR US TO WITH-DRAW.
BE-SIDES, THIS POKÉ-MON SEEMS TO BE...
...TRYING TO LURE US DEEPER INTO THE BUILDING.
IF IT DOESN'T WANT PEOPLE ENTERING ITS TERRITORY, IT WOULD HAVE ATTACKED US THE MOMENT WE ENTERED.
SO WHY DID IT GET MAD AND ATTACK US NOW?

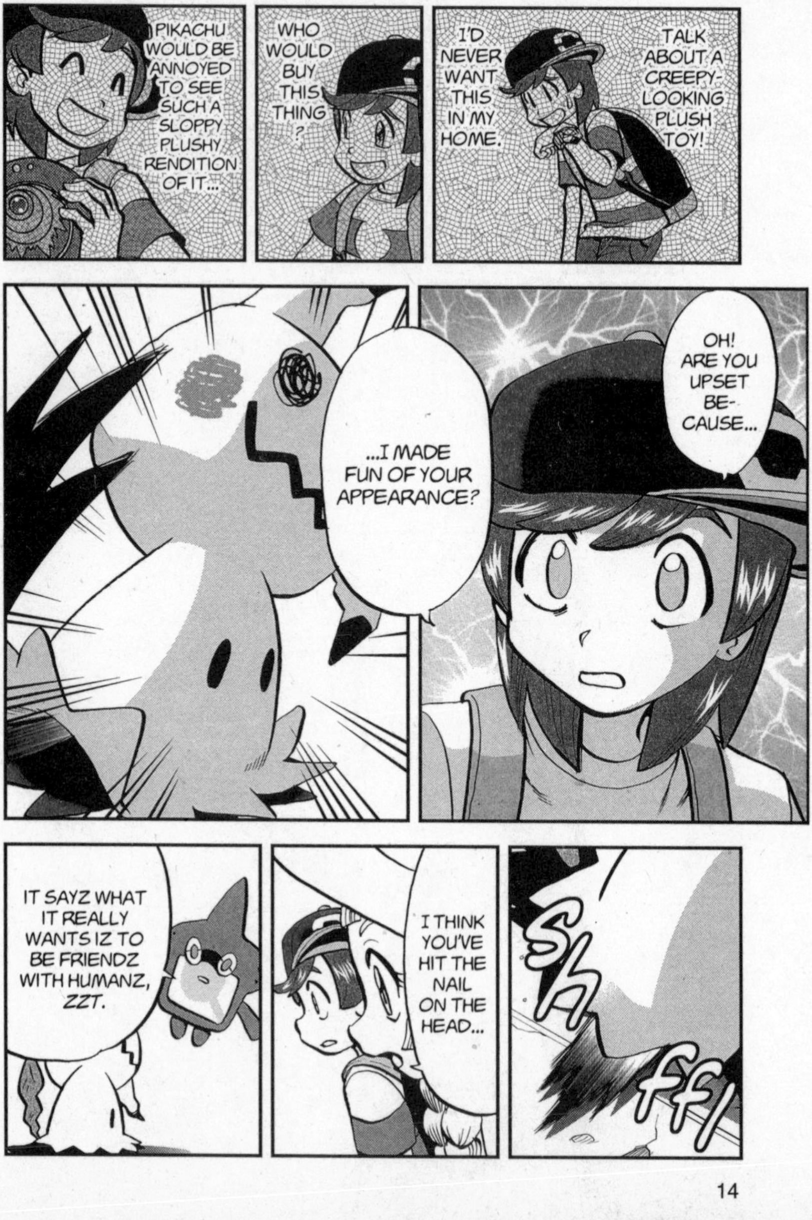
TALK ABOUT A CREEPY-LOOKING PLUSH TOY!
I'D NEVER WANT THIS IN MY HOME.
WHO WOULD BUY THIS THING?
PIKACHU WOULD BE ANNOYED TO SEE SUCH A SLOPPY PLUSHY RENDITION OF IT...
OH! ARE YOU UPSET BE-CAUSE...
...I MADE FUN OF YOUR APPEARANCE?
SHFF!
I THINK YOU'VE HIT THE NAIL ON THE HEAD...
IT SAYZ WHAT IT REALLY WANTS IZ TO BE FRIENDZ WITH HUMANZ, ZZT.

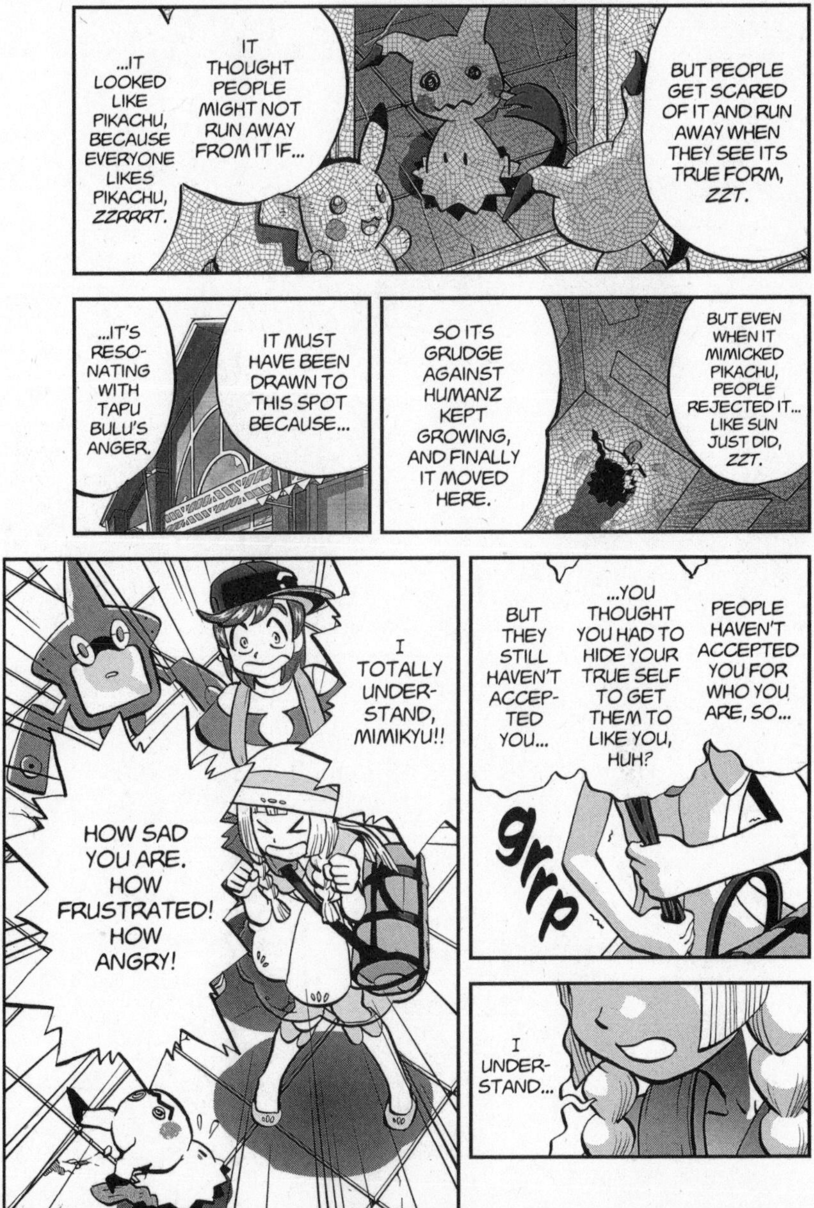
BUT PEOPLE GET SCARED OF IT AND RUN AWAY WHEN THEY SEE ITS TRUE FORM, ZZT.
IT THOUGHT PEOPLE MIGHT NOT RUN AWAY FROM IT IF...
...IT LOOKED LIKE PIKACHU, BECAUSE EVERYONE LIKES PIKACHU, ZZRRRT.
BUT EVEN WHEN IT MIMICKED PIKACHU, PEOPLE REJECTED IT... LIKE SUN JUST DID, ZZT.
SO ITS GRUDGE AGAINST HUMANZ KEPT GROWING, AND FINALLY IT MOVED HERE.
IT MUST HAVE BEEN DRAWN TO THIS SPOT BECAUSE...
...IT'S RESONATING WITH TAPU BULU'S ANGER.
PEOPLE HAVEN'T ACCEPTED YOU FOR WHO YOU ARE, SO...
...YOU THOUGHT YOU HAD TO HIDE YOUR TRUE SELF TO GET THEM TO LIKE YOU, HUH?
BUT THEY STILL HAVEN'T ACCEPTED YOU...
grrp
I UNDERSTAND...
I TOTALLY UNDERSTAND, MIMIKYU!!
HOW SAD YOU ARE. HOW FRUSTRATED! HOW ANGRY!

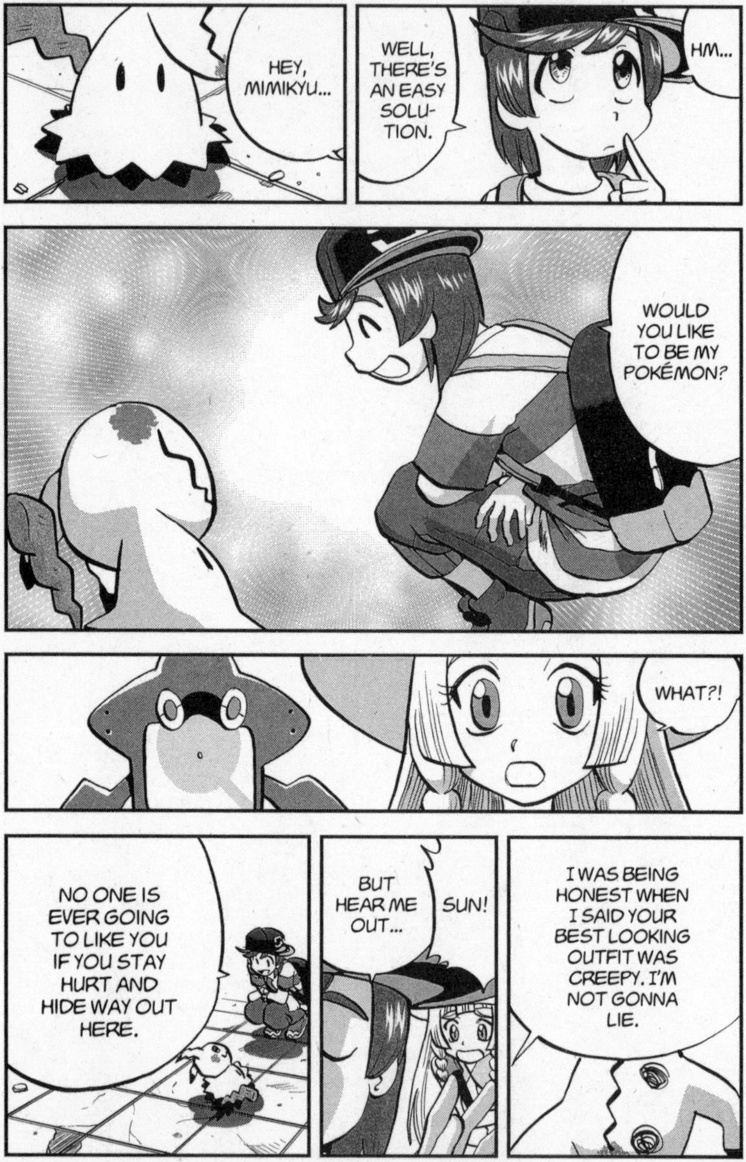
HM...
WELL, THERE'S AN EASY SOLU- TION.
HEY, MIMIKYU...
WOULD YOU LIKE TO BE MY POKÉMON?
WHAT?!
I WAS BEING HONEST WHEN I SAID YOUR BEST LOOKING OUTFIT WAS CREEPY. I'M NOT GONNA LIE.
SUN!
BUT HEAR ME OUT...
NO ONE IS EVER GOING TO LIKE YOU IF YOU STAY HURT AND HIDE WAY OUT HERE.

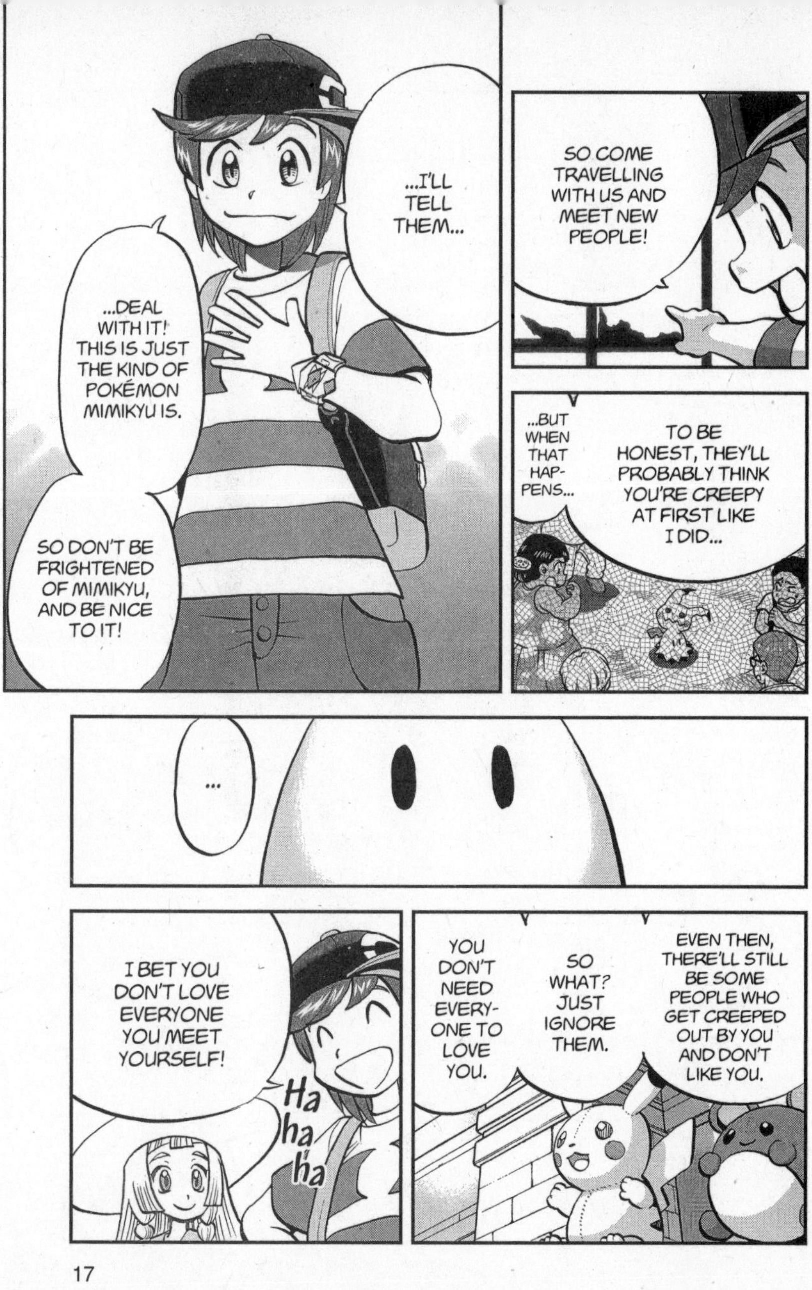
SO COME TRAVELLING WITH US AND MEET NEW PEOPLE!
TO BE HONEST, THEY'LL PROBABLY THINK YOU'RE CREEPY AT FIRST LIKE I DID...
...BUT WHEN THAT HAP-PENS...
...I'LL TELL THEM...
...DEAL WITH IT! THIS IS JUST THE KIND OF POKÉMON MIMIKYU IS.
SO DON'T BE FRIGHTENED OF MIMIKYU, AND BE NICE TO IT!
...
EVEN THEN, THERE'LL STILL BE SOME PEOPLE WHO GET CREEPED OUT BY YOU AND DON'T LIKE YOU.
SO WHAT? JUST IGNORE THEM.
YOU DON'T NEED EVERY-ONE TO LOVE YOU.
I BET YOU DON'T LOVE EVERYONE YOU MEET YOURSELF!
Ha ha ha ha

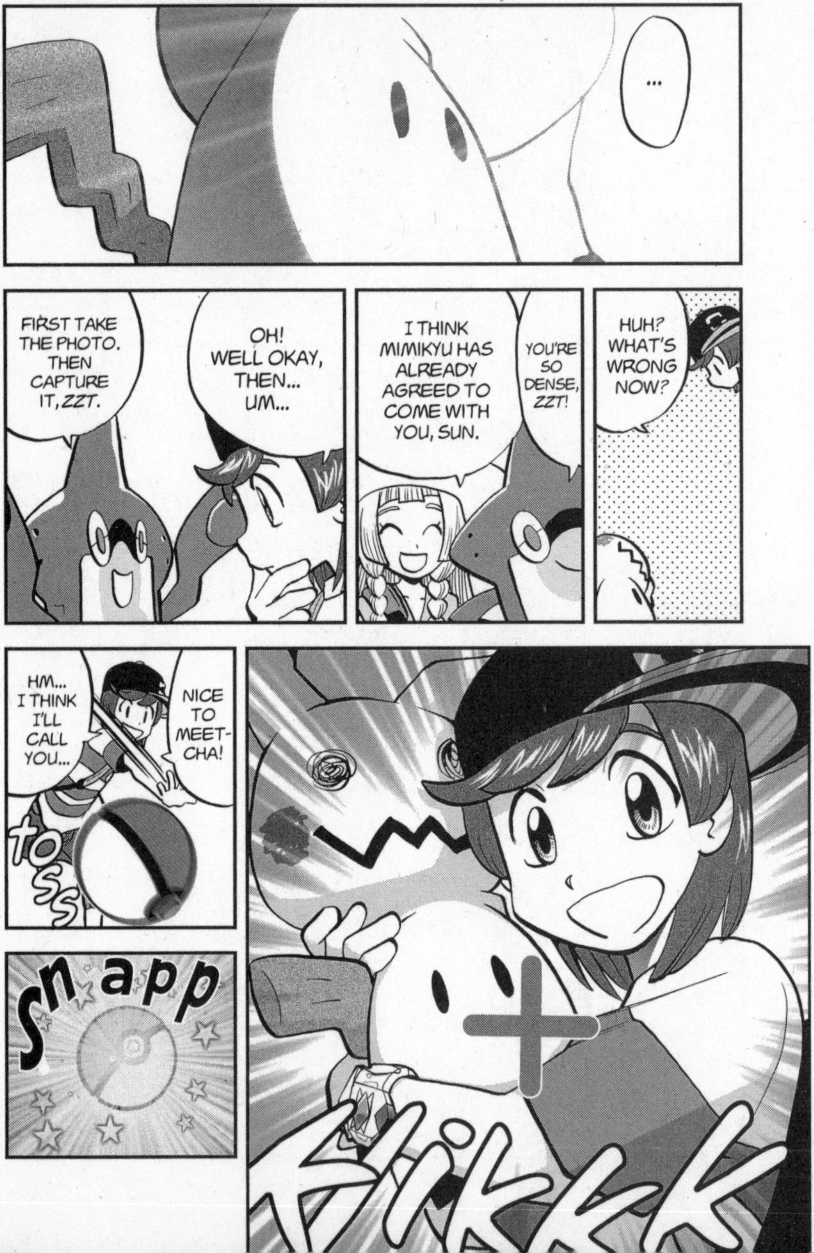
...
HUH? WHAT'S WRONG NOW?
YOU'RE SO DENSE, ZZT!
I THINK MIMIKYU HAS ALREADY AGREED TO COME WITH YOU, SUN.
OH! WELL OKAY, THEN... UM...
FIRST TAKE THE PHOTO. THEN CAPTURE IT, ZZT.
FLIKKK
NICE TO MEET-CHA!
HM... I THINK I'LL CALL YOU...
TOSS
SNAPP

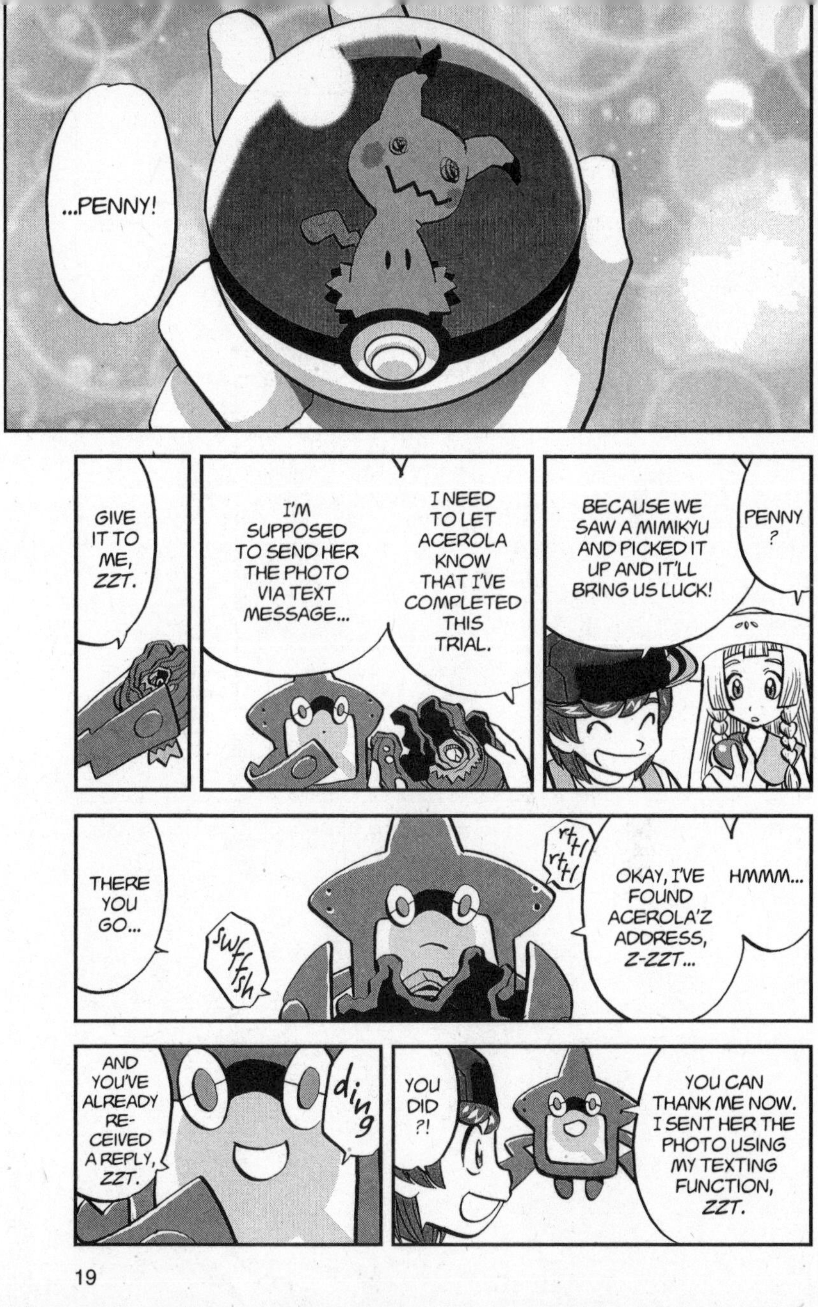
...PENNY!
PENNY?
BECAUSE WE SAW A MIMIKYU AND PICKED IT UP AND IT'LL BRING US LUCK!
I NEED TO LET ACEROLA KNOW THAT I'VE COMPLETED THIS TRIAL.
I'M SUPPOSED TO SEND HER THE PHOTO VIA TEXT MESSAGE...
GIVE IT TO ME, ZZT.
HMMM...
OKAY, I'VE FOUND ACEROLA'Z ADDRESS, Z-ZZT...
rttl rttl
swffsh
THERE YOU GO...
YOU CAN THANK ME NOW. I SENT HER THE PHOTO USING MY TEXTING FUNCTION, ZZT.
YOU DID?!
ding
AND YOU'VE ALREADY RE-CEIVED A REPLY, ZZT.

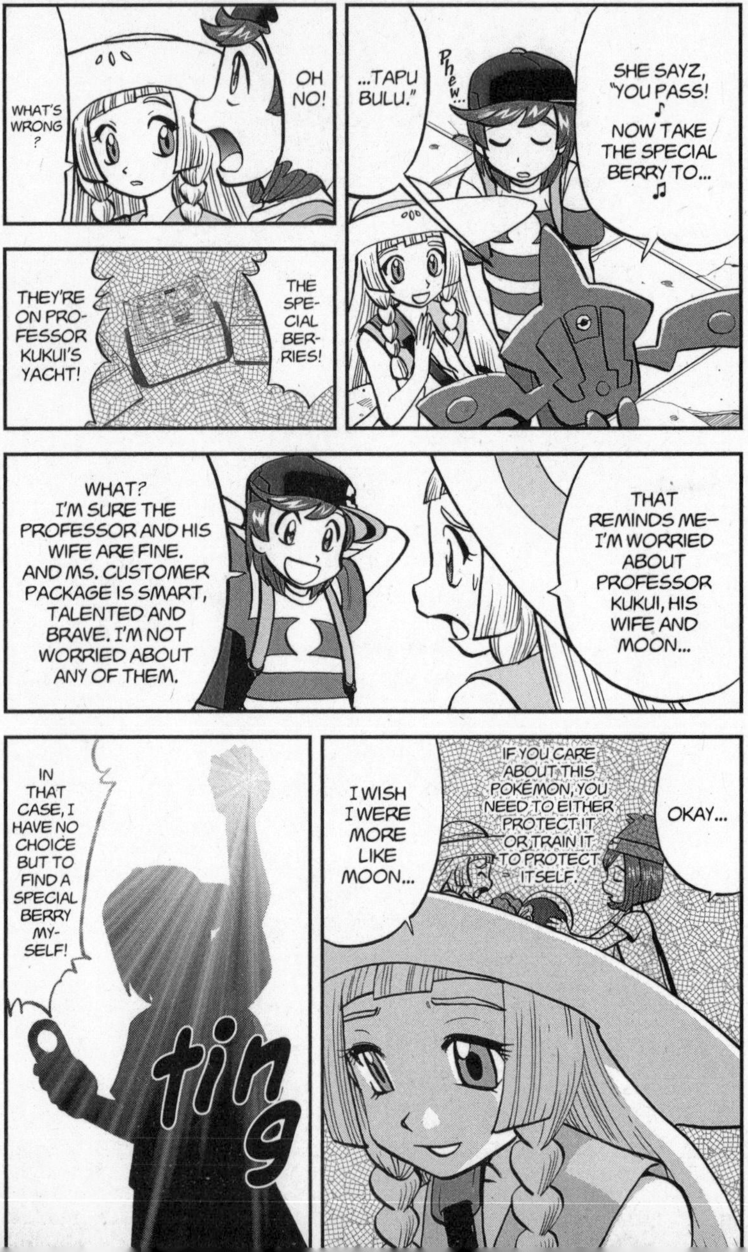
SHE SAYZ, "YOU PASS! ♪ NOW TAKE THE SPECIAL BERRY TO... ♫
Phew...
...TAPU BULU."
OH NO!
WHAT'S WRONG?
THE SPECIAL BERRIES!
THEY'RE ON PROFESSOR KUKUI'S YACHT!
THAT REMINDS ME—I'M WORRIED ABOUT PROFESSOR KUKUI, HIS WIFE AND MOON...
WHAT? I'M SURE THE PROFESSOR AND HIS WIFE ARE FINE. AND MS. CUSTOMER PACKAGE IS SMART, TALENTED AND BRAVE. I'M NOT WORRIED ABOUT ANY OF THEM.
OKAY...
IF YOU CARE ABOUT THIS POKÉMON, YOU NEED TO EITHER PROTECT IT OR TRAIN IT TO PROTECT ITSELF.
I WISH I WERE MORE LIKE MOON...
IN THAT CASE, I HAVE NO CHOICE BUT TO FIND A SPECIAL BERRY MYSELF!
ting

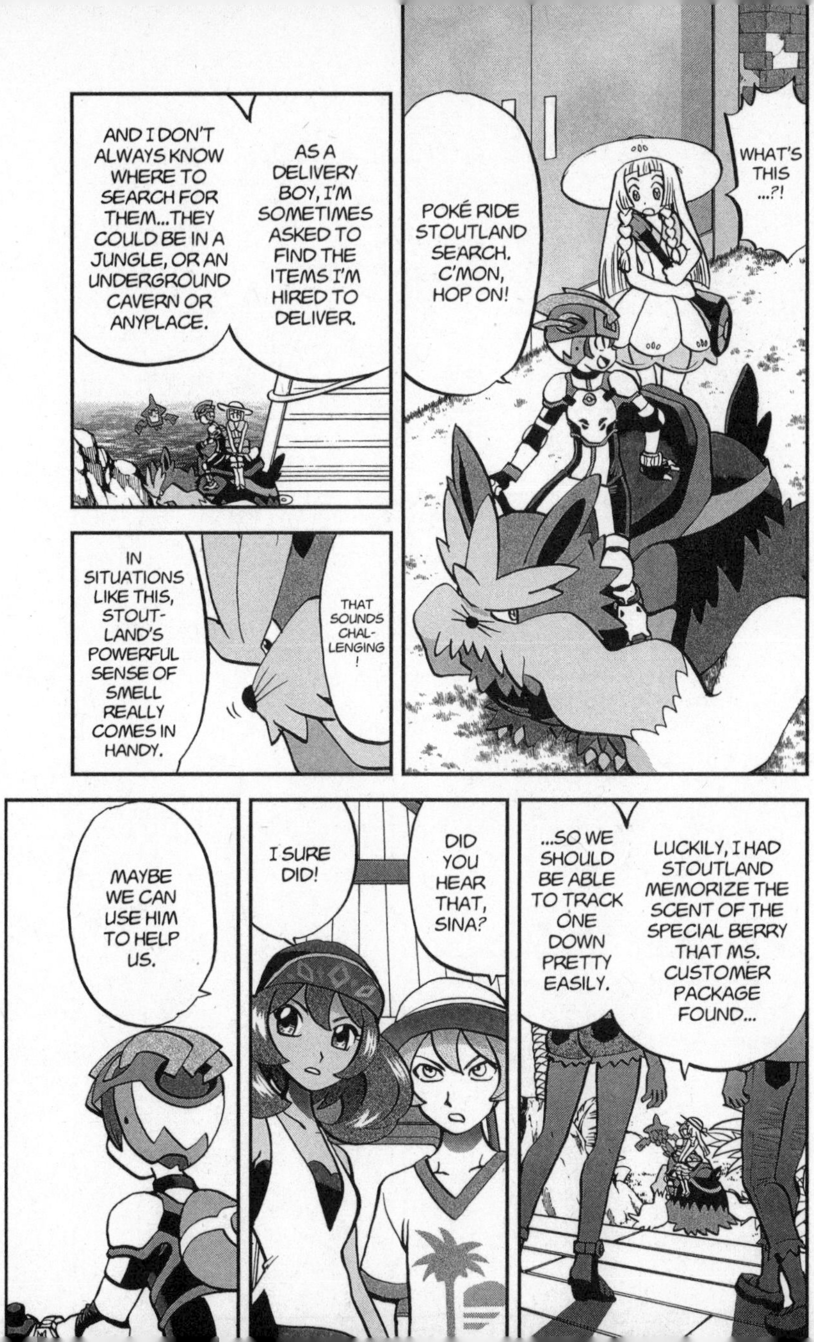
WHAT'S THIS ...?!
POKÉ RIDE STOUTLAND SEARCH. C'MON, HOP ON!
AS A DELIVERY BOY, I'M SOMETIMES ASKED TO FIND THE ITEMS I'M HIRED TO DELIVER.
AND I DON'T ALWAYS KNOW WHERE TO SEARCH FOR THEM...THEY COULD BE IN A JUNGLE, OR AN UNDERGROUND CAVERN OR ANYPLACE.
THAT SOUNDS CHAL-LENGING!
IN SITUATIONS LIKE THIS, STOUT-LAND'S POWERFUL SENSE OF SMELL REALLY COMES IN HANDY.
LUCKILY, I HAD STOUTLAND MEMORIZE THE SCENT OF THE SPECIAL BERRY THAT MS. CUSTOMER PACKAGE FOUND...
...SO WE SHOULD BE ABLE TO TRACK ONE DOWN PRETTY EASILY.
DID YOU HEAR THAT, SINA?
I SURE DID!
MAYBE WE CAN USE HIM TO HELP US.

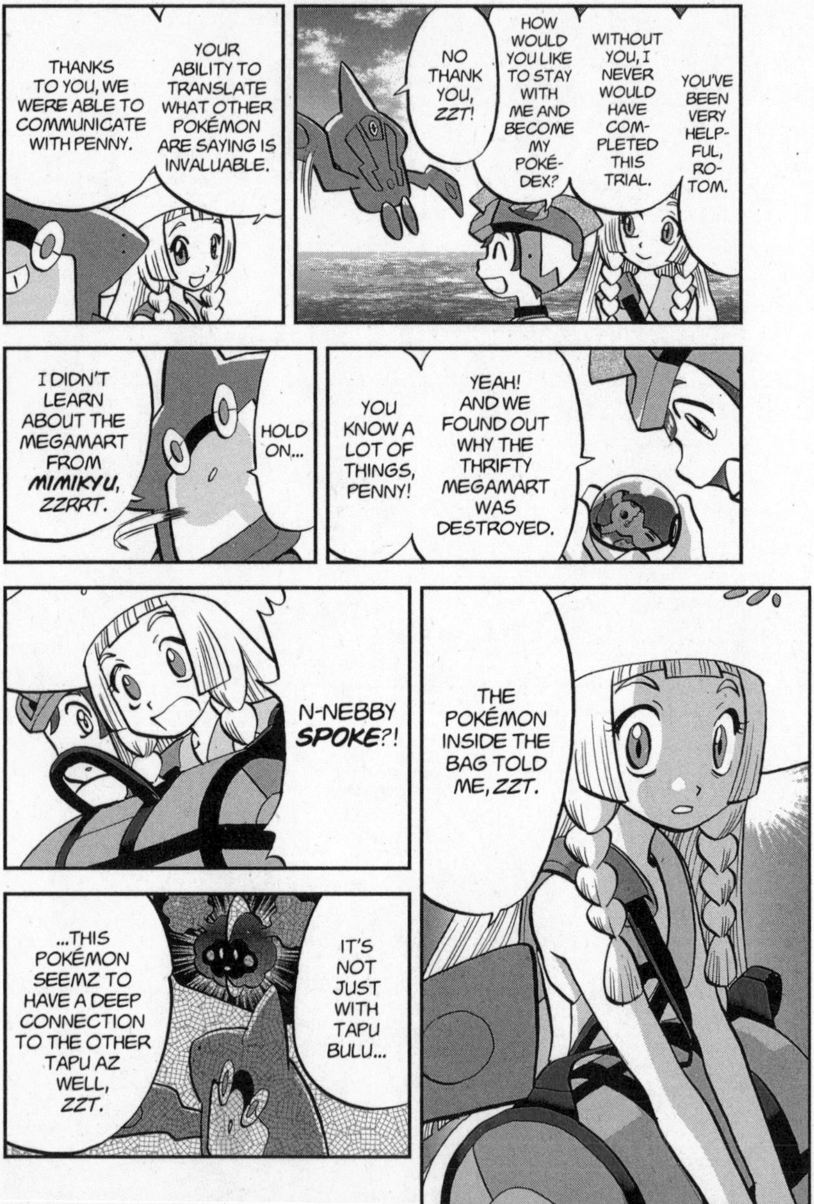
YOU'VE BEEN VERY HELPFUL, ROTOM.
WITHOUT YOU, I NEVER WOULD HAVE COMPLETED THIS TRIAL.
HOW WOULD YOU LIKE TO STAY WITH ME AND BECOME MY POKÉDEX?
NO THANK YOU, ZZT!
YOUR ABILITY TO TRANSLATE WHAT OTHER POKÉMON ARE SAYING IS INVALUABLE.
THANKS TO YOU, WE WERE ABLE TO COMMUNICATE WITH PENNY.
YEAH! AND WE FOUND OUT WHY THE THRIFTY MEGAMART WAS DESTROYED.
YOU KNOW A LOT OF THINGS, PENNY!
HOLD ON...
I DIDN'T LEARN ABOUT THE MEGAMART FROM MIMIKYU, ZZRRT.
THE POKÉMON INSIDE THE BAG TOLD ME, ZZT.
N-NEBBY SPOKE?!
IT'S NOT JUST WITH TAPU BULU...
...THIS POKÉMON SEEMZ TO HAVE A DEEP CONNECTION TO THE OTHER TAPU AZ WELL, ZZT.

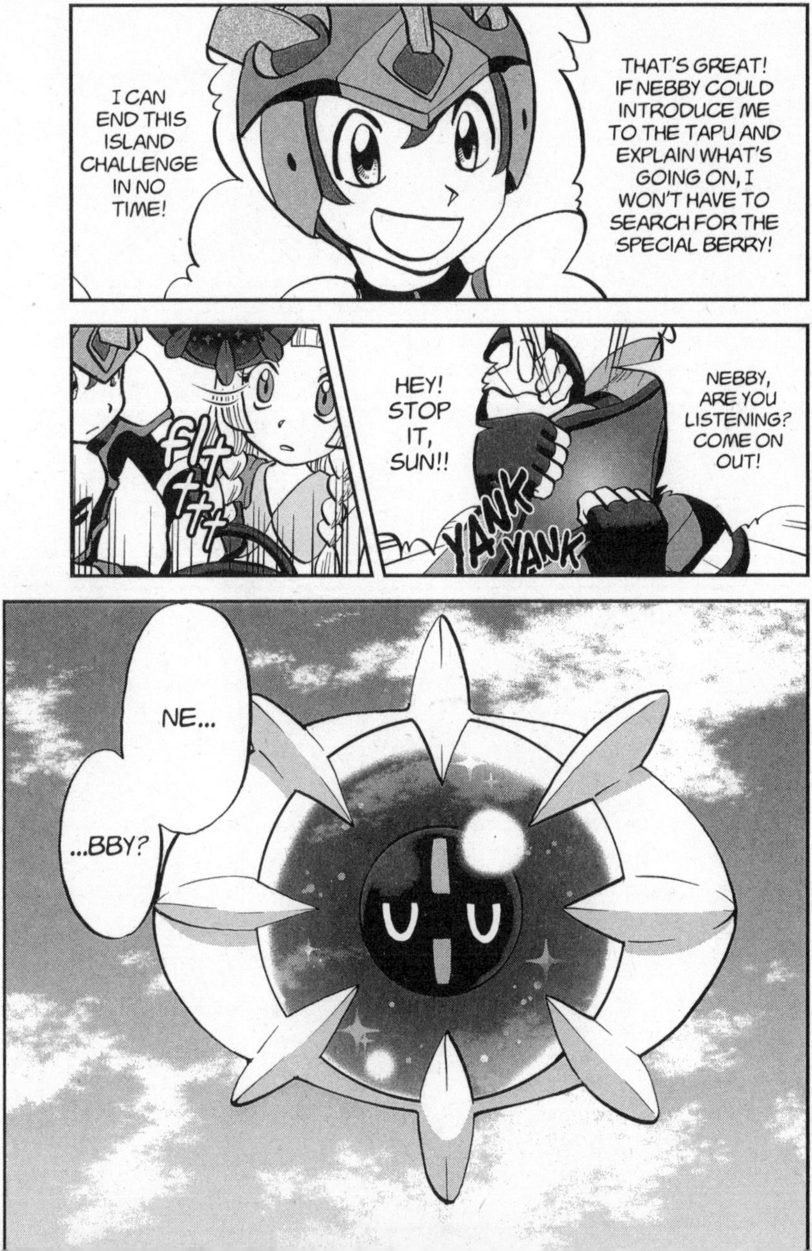
THAT'S GREAT! IF NEBBY COULD INTRODUCE ME TO THE TAPU AND EXPLAIN WHAT'S GOING ON, I WON'T HAVE TO SEARCH FOR THE SPECIAL BERRY!
I CAN END THIS ISLAND CHALLENGE IN NO TIME!
NEBBY, ARE YOU LISTENING? COME ON OUT!
HEY! STOP IT, SUN!!
YANK
YANK
NE...
...BBY?

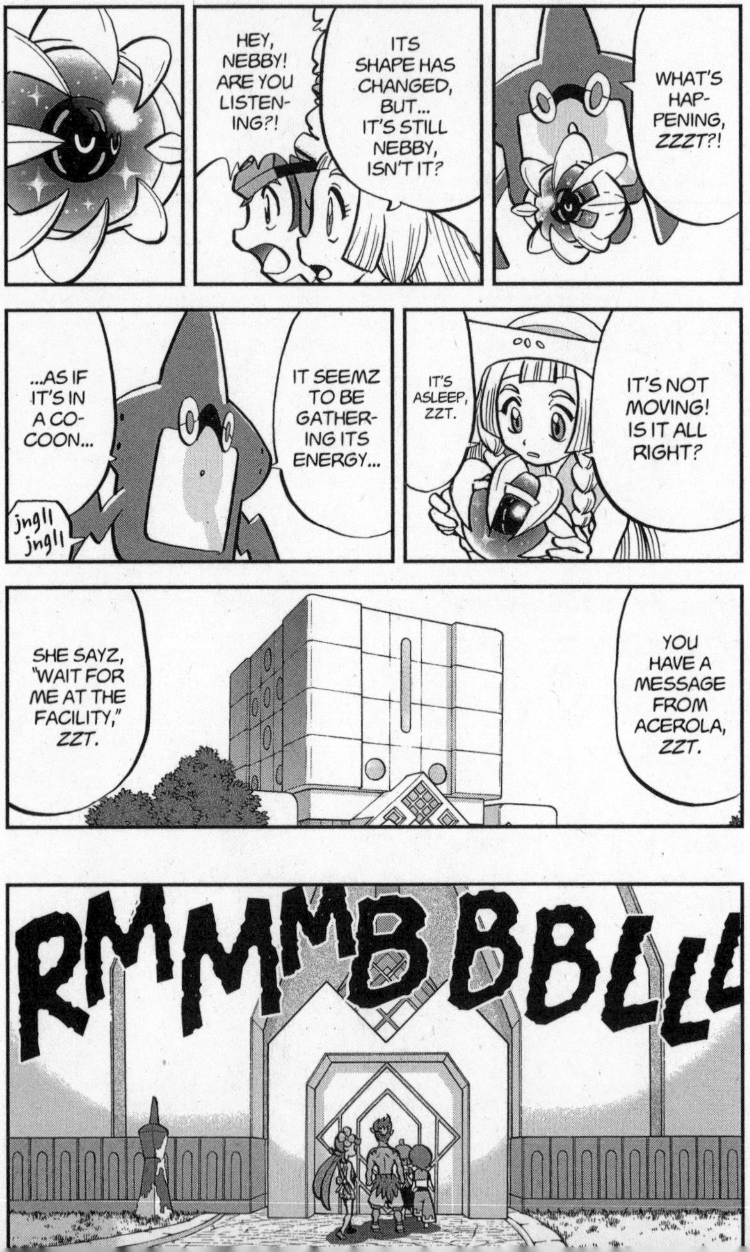
WHAT'S HAP-PENING, ZZZT?!
ITS SHAPE HAS CHANGED, BUT... IT'S STILL NEBBY, ISN'T IT?
HEY, NEBBY! ARE YOU LISTEN-ING?!
IT'S NOT MOVING! IS IT ALL RIGHT?
IT'S ASLEEP, ZZT.
IT SEEMZ TO BE GATHER-ING ITS ENERGY...
...AS IF IT'S IN A CO-COON...
jngll jngll
YOU HAVE A MESSAGE FROM ACEROLA, ZZT.
SHE SAYZ, "WAIT FOR ME AT THE FACILITY," ZZT.
RMMMBBBLL

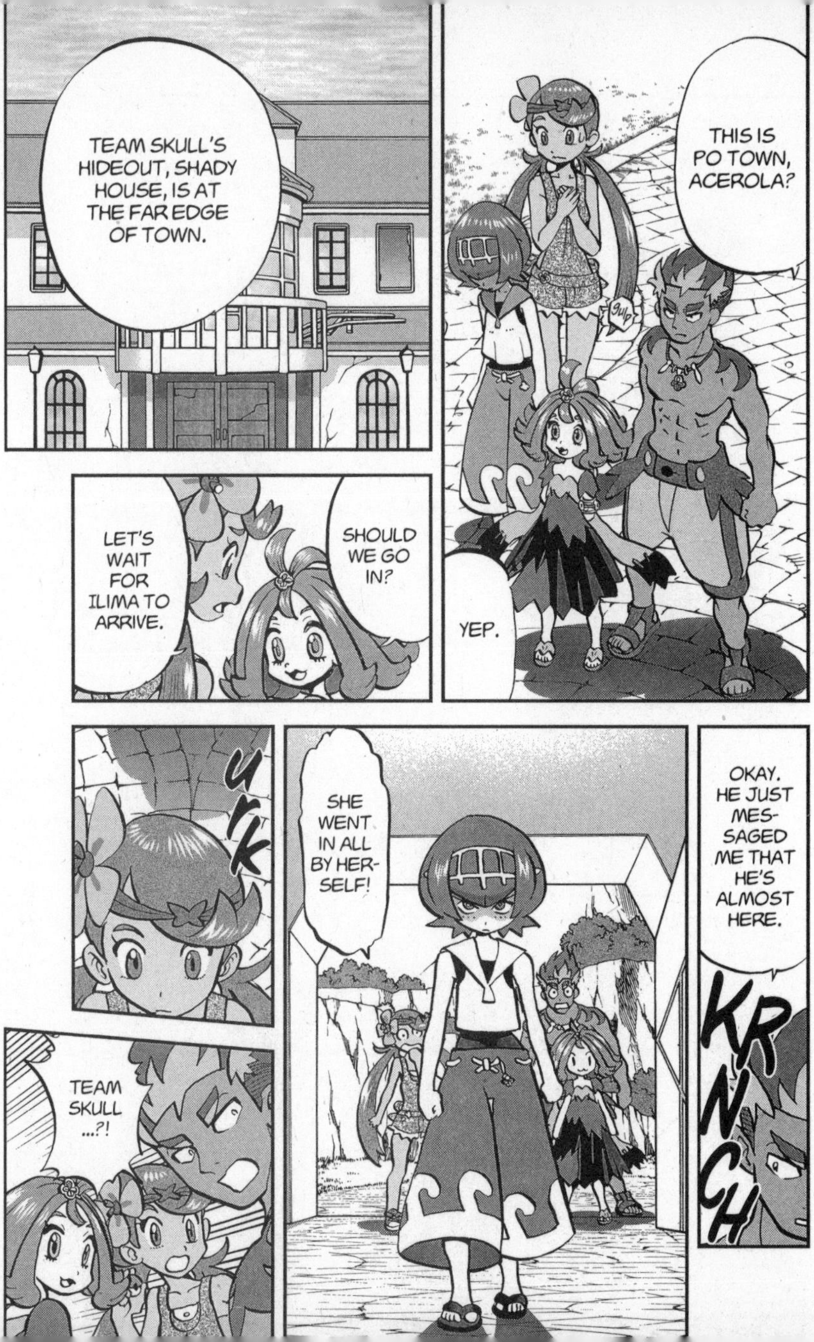
THIS IS PO TOWN, ACEROLA?
gulp
YEP.
TEAM SKULL'S HIDEOUT, SHADY HOUSE, IS AT THE FAR EDGE OF TOWN.
SHOULD WE GO IN?
LET'S WAIT FOR ILIMA TO ARRIVE.
OKAY. HE JUST MES-SAGED ME THAT HE'S ALMOST HERE.
KRNCH
SHE WENT IN ALL BY HER-SELF!
urk
TEAM SKULL ...?!

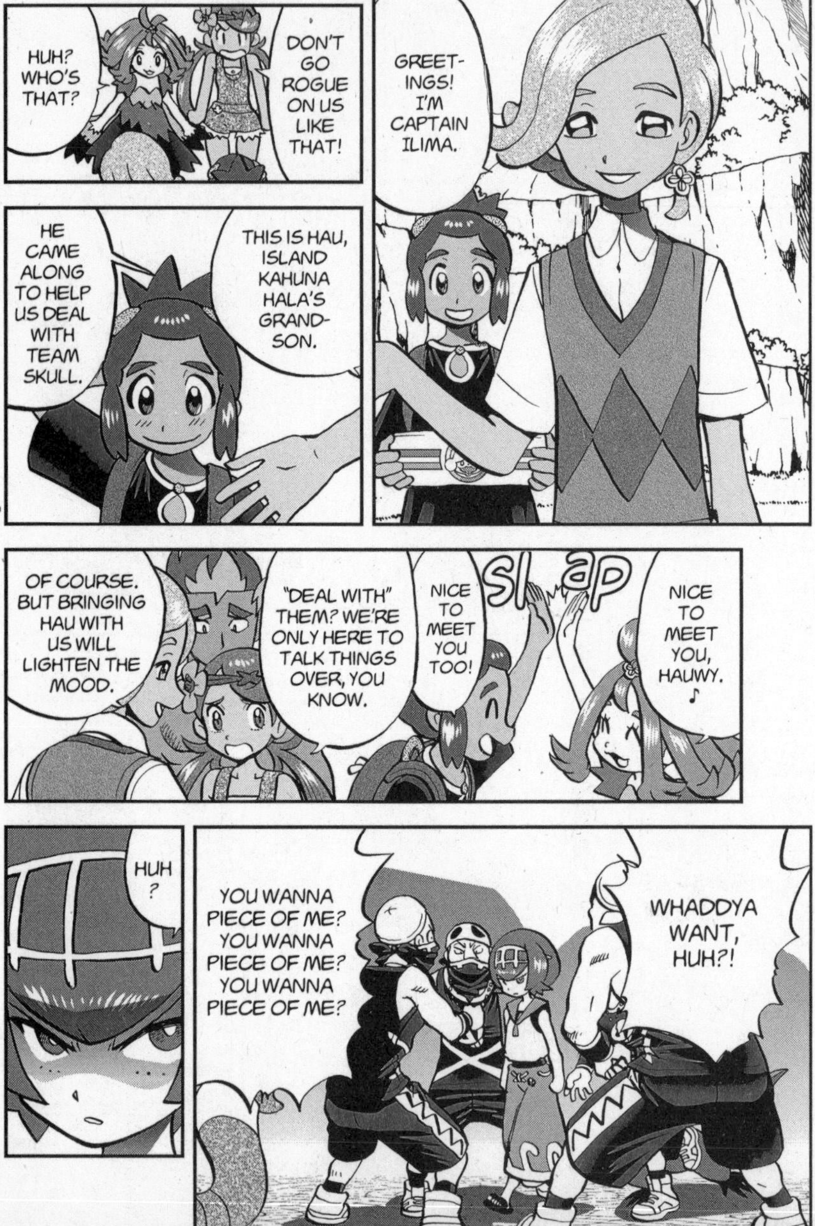
GREETINGS! I'M CAPTAIN ILIMA.
DON'T GO ROGUE ON US LIKE THAT!
HUH? WHO'S THAT?
THIS IS HAU, ISLAND KAHUNA HALA'S GRANDSON.
HE CAME ALONG TO HELP US DEAL WITH TEAM SKULL.
NICE TO MEET YOU, HAUWY. ♪
SLAP
NICE TO MEET YOU TOO!
"DEAL WITH" THEM? WE'RE ONLY HERE TO TALK THINGS OVER, YOU KNOW.
OF COURSE. BUT BRINGING HAU WITH US WILL LIGHTEN THE MOOD.
WHADDYA WANT, HUH?!
YOU WANNA PIECE OF ME? YOU WANNA PIECE OF ME? YOU WANNA PIECE OF ME?
HUH?

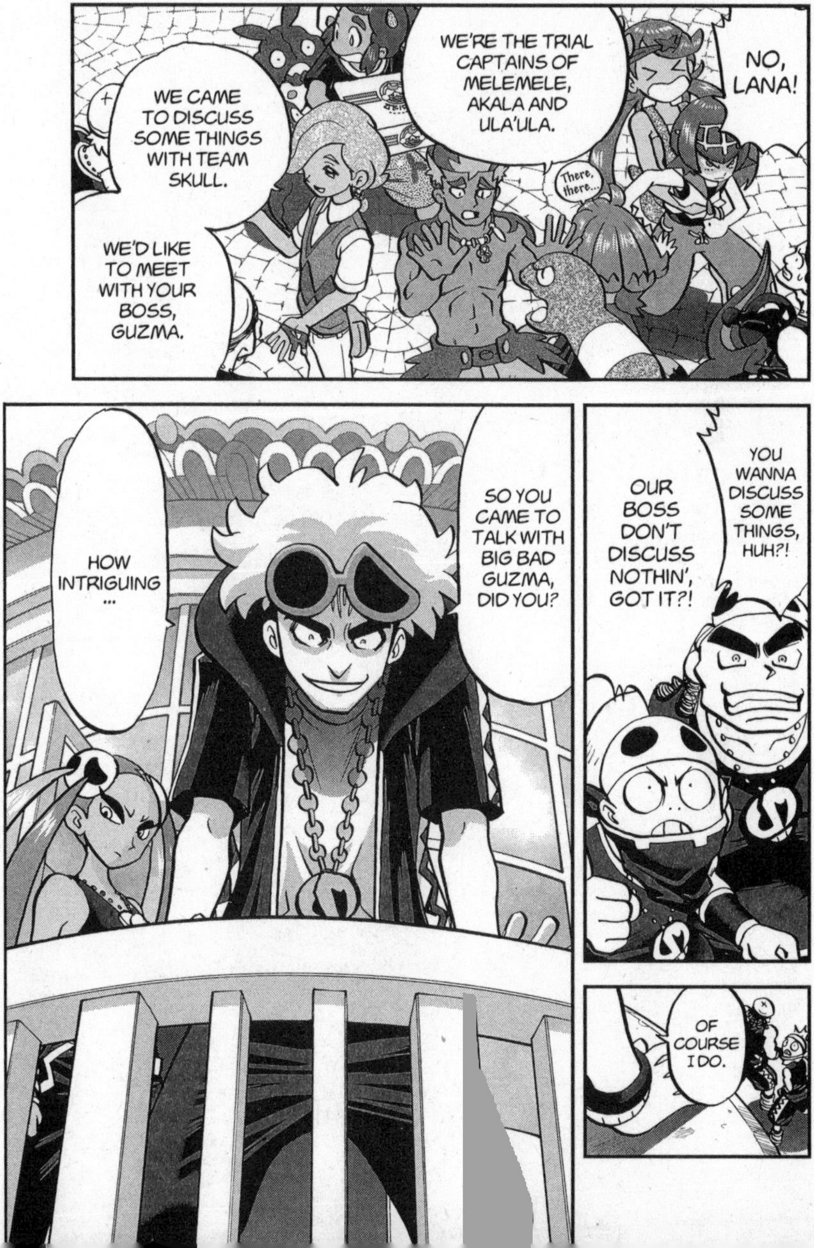
NO, LANA!
WE'RE THE TRIAL CAPTAINS OF MELEMELE, AKALA AND ULA'ULA.
There, there...
WE CAME TO DISCUSS SOME THINGS WITH TEAM SKULL.
WE'D LIKE TO MEET WITH YOUR BOSS, GUZMA.
YOU WANNA DISCUSS SOME THINGS, HUH?!
OUR BOSS DON'T DISCUSS NOTHIN', GOT IT?!
OF COURSE I DO.
SO YOU CAME TO TALK WITH BIG BAD GUZMA, DID YOU?
HOW INTRIGUING ...

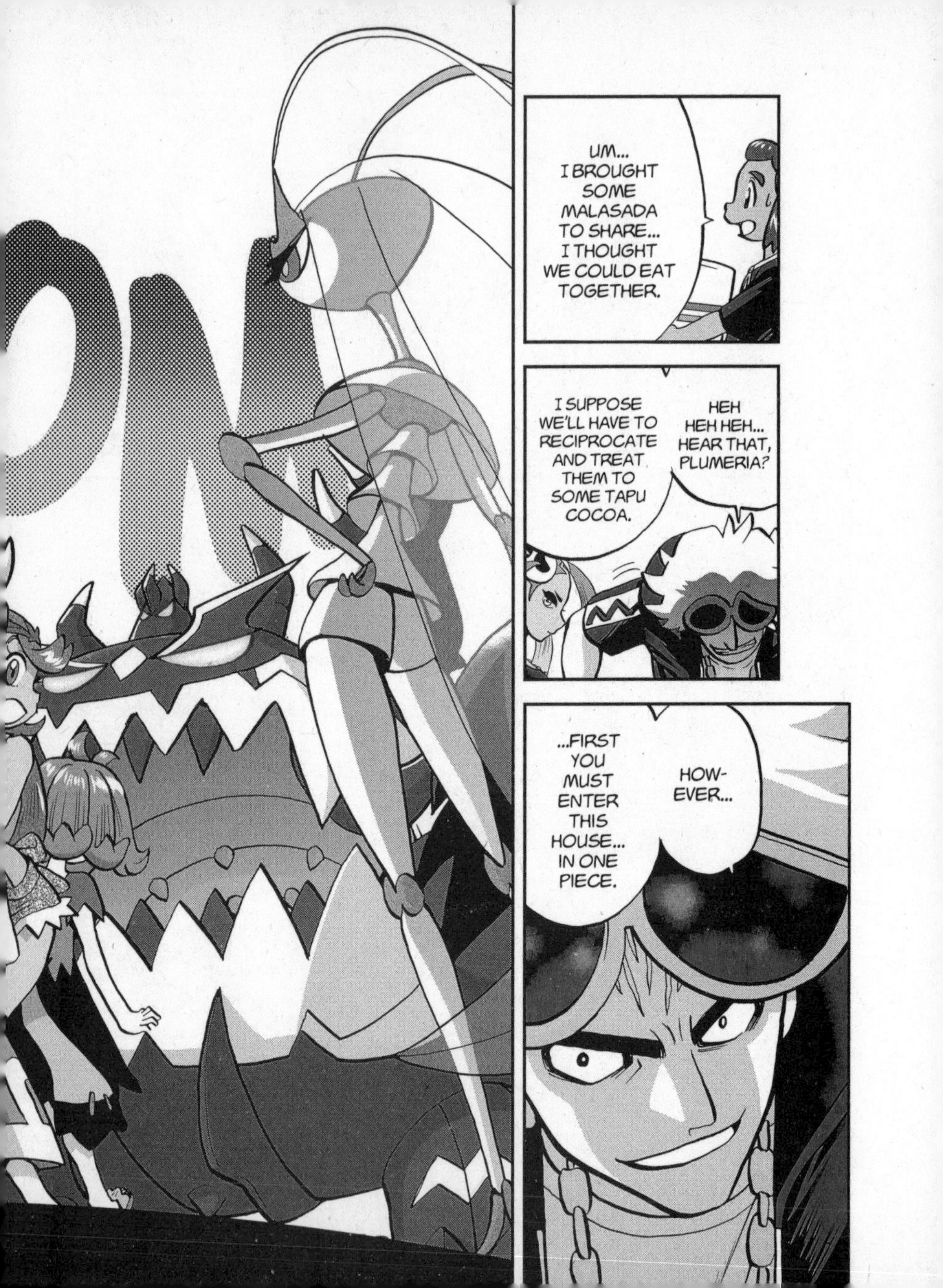
UM... I BROUGHT SOME MALASADA TO SHARE... I THOUGHT WE COULD EAT TOGETHER.
HEH HEH HEH... HEAR THAT, PLUMERIA?
I SUPPOSE WE'LL HAVE TO RECIPROCATE AND TREAT THEM TO SOME TAPU COCOA.
HOW-EVER...
...FIRST YOU MUST ENTER THIS HOUSE... IN ONE PIECE.

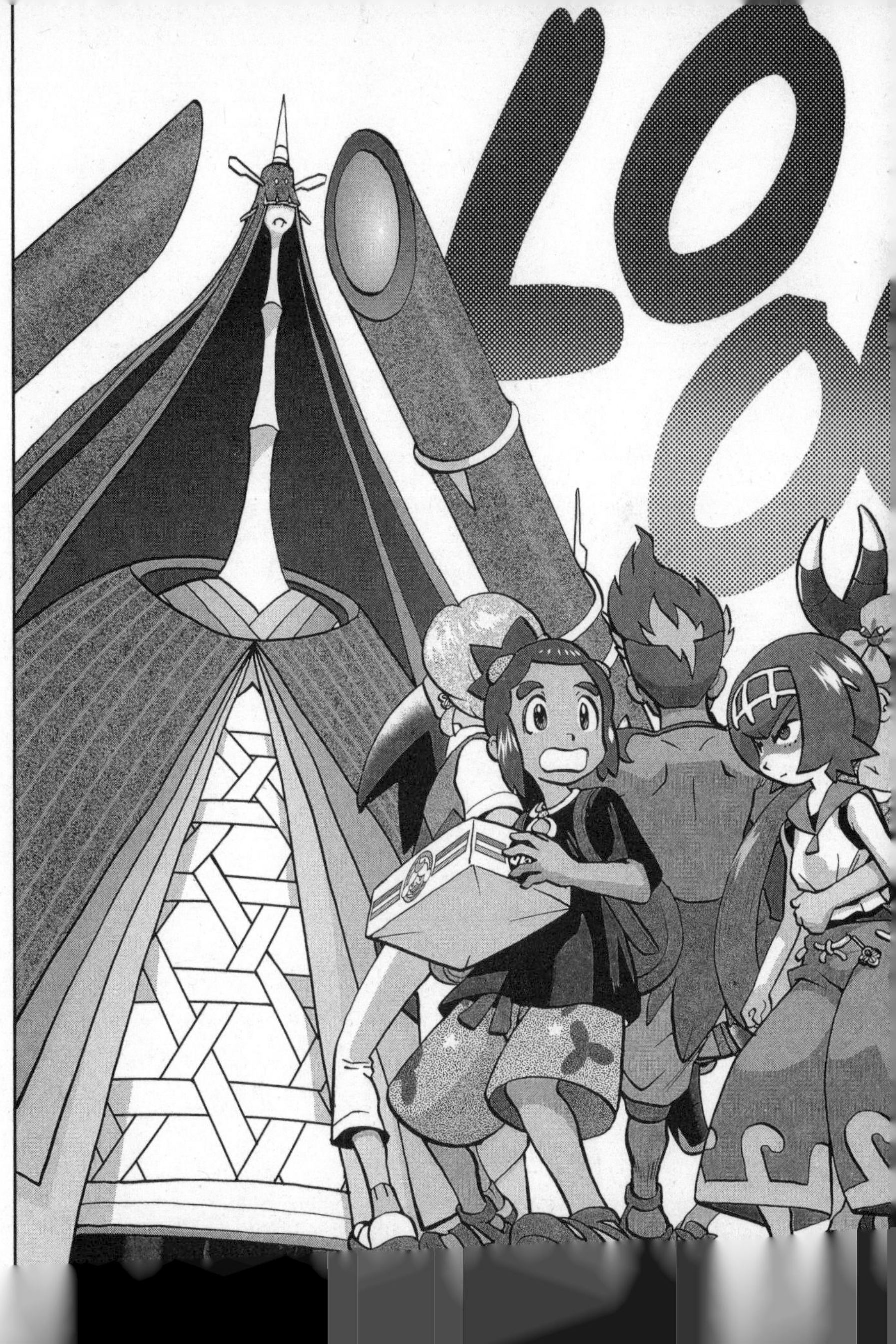
LO
O

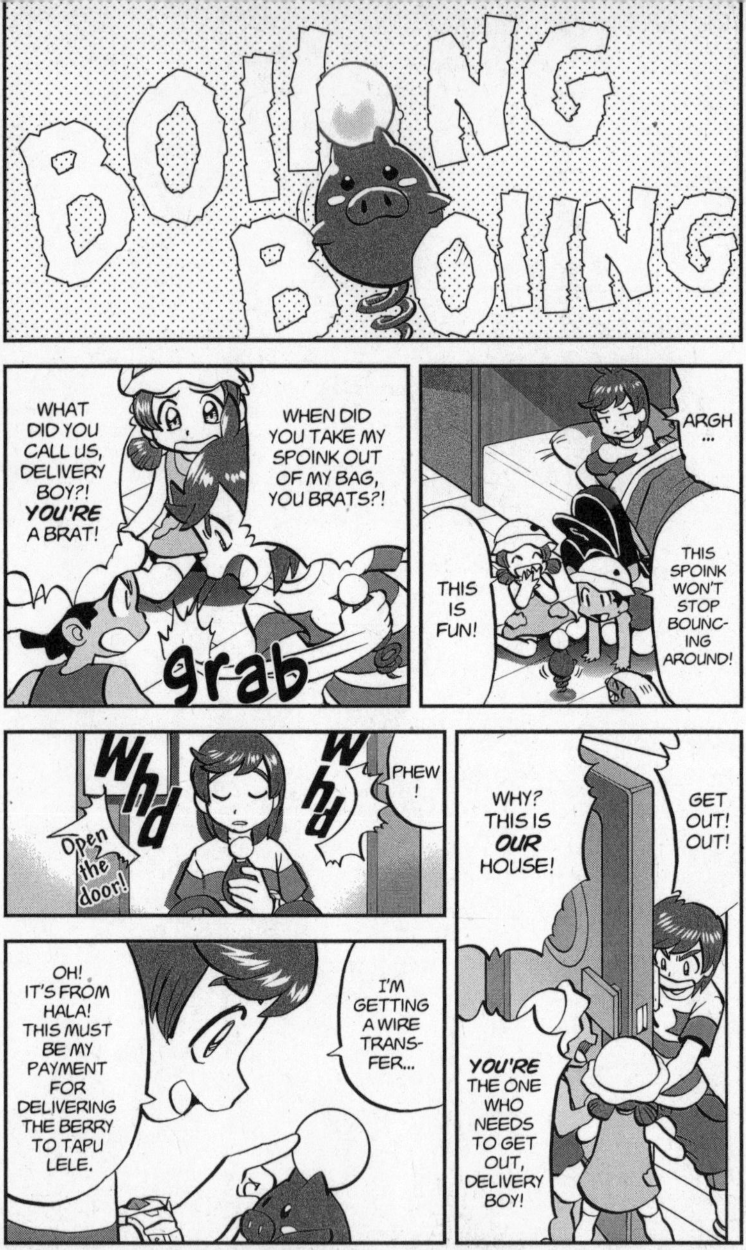
BOIING
BOIING
ARGH...
THIS SPOINK WON'T STOP BOUNC-ING AROUND!
THIS IS FUN!
WHEN DID YOU TAKE MY SPOINK OUT OF MY BAG, YOU BRATS?!
WHAT DID YOU CALL US, DELIVERY BOY?! ***YOU'RE*** A BRAT!
grab
GET OUT! OUT!
WHY? THIS IS ***OUR*** HOUSE!
YOU'RE THE ONE WHO NEEDS TO GET OUT, DELIVERY BOY!
Whd
Whd
PHEW!
Open the door!
I'M GETTING A WIRE TRANS-FER...
OH! IT'S FROM HALA! THIS MUST BE MY PAYMENT FOR DELIVERING THE BERRY TO TAPU LELE.

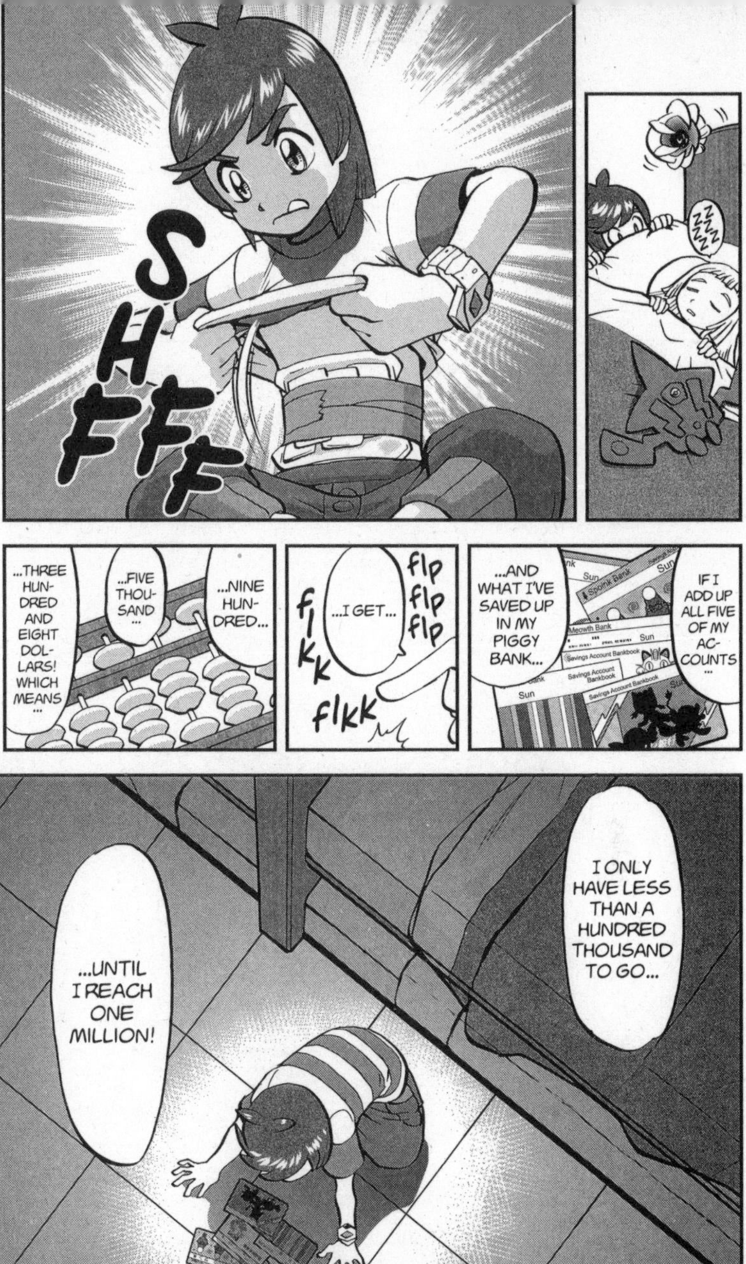
ZZZZZZ
SHFFF
IF I ADD UP ALL FIVE OF MY ACCOUNTS...
...AND WHAT I'VE SAVED UP IN MY PIGGY BANK...
Spoink Bank
Meowth Bank
Savings Account Bankbook
Sun
flp flp flp
...I GET...
flkk
flkk
...NINE HUNDRED...
...FIVE THOUSAND...
...THREE HUNDRED AND EIGHT DOLLARS! WHICH MEANS...
I ONLY HAVE LESS THAN A HUNDRED THOUSAND TO GO...
...UNTIL I REACH ONE MILLION!

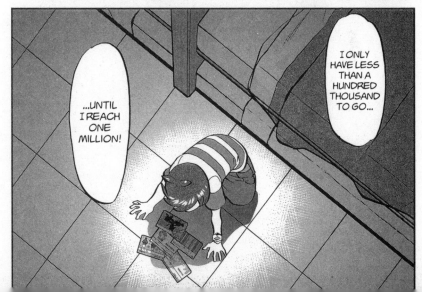

Call for Help

In battle against a wild Pokémon, your opponent might call for help from a fellow Pokémon. It can be devastating when your opponent brings in backup when you are already in over your head...

Guide to Alola 15

Adventure 18
Confusion and Monsters from Another World

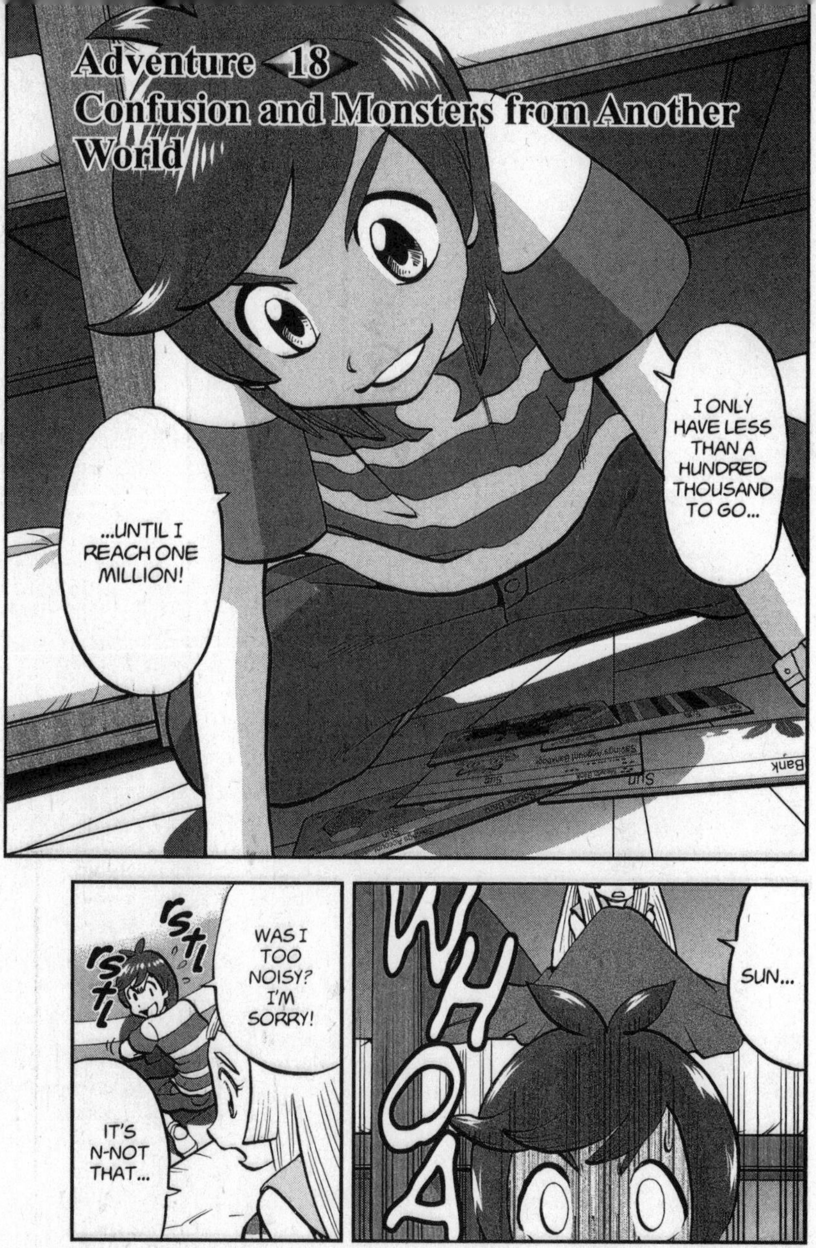
I ONLY HAVE LESS THAN A HUNDRED THOUSAND TO GO...
...UNTIL I REACH ONE MILLION!
Bank
Sun
SUN...
WHOA
rstl rstl
WAS I TOO NOISY? I'M SORRY!
IT'S N-NOT THAT...

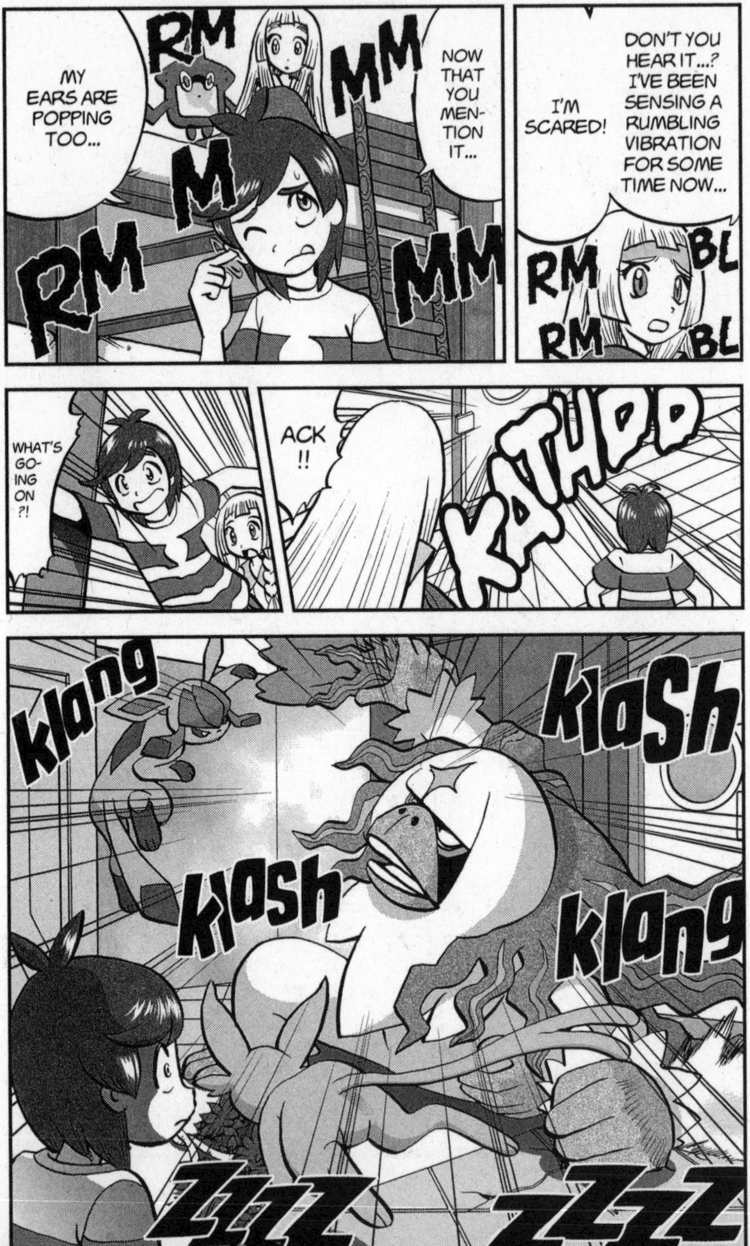
DON'T YOU HEAR IT...? I'VE BEEN SENSING A RUMBLING VIBRATION FOR SOME TIME NOW...
I'M SCARED!
RM RM
BL BL
NOW THAT YOU MEN-TION IT...
MY EARS ARE POPPING TOO...
RM MM M RM MM
KATHOD
ACK !!
WHAT'S GO-ING ON ?!
klash
klang
klang
klash
ZZZ
ZZZ

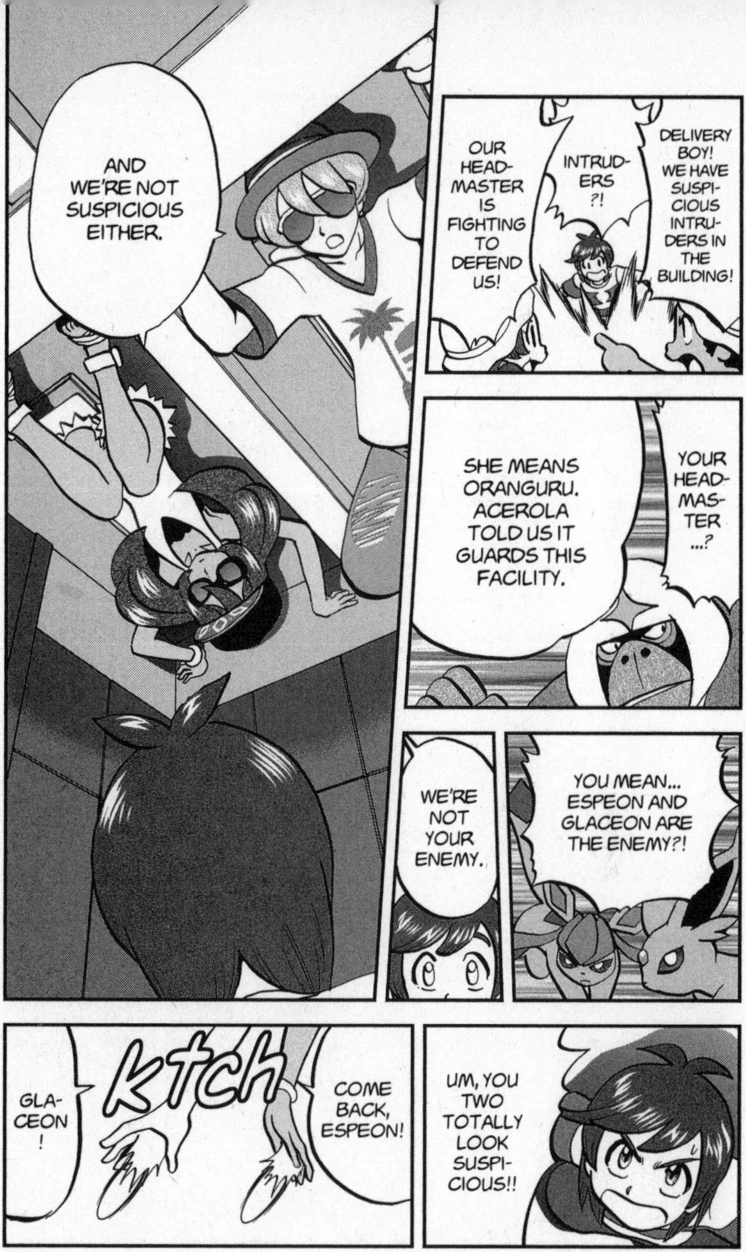
DELIVERY BOY! WE HAVE SUSPICIOUS INTRUDERS IN THE BUILDING!
INTRUDERS?!
OUR HEADMASTER IS FIGHTING TO DEFEND US!
YOUR HEADMASTER...?
SHE MEANS ORANGURU. ACEROLA TOLD US IT GUARDS THIS FACILITY.
YOU MEAN... ESPEON AND GLACEON ARE THE ENEMY?!
WE'RE NOT YOUR ENEMY.
AND WE'RE NOT SUSPICIOUS EITHER.
UM, YOU TWO TOTALLY LOOK SUSPICIOUS!!
COME BACK, ESPEON!
ktch
GLACEON!

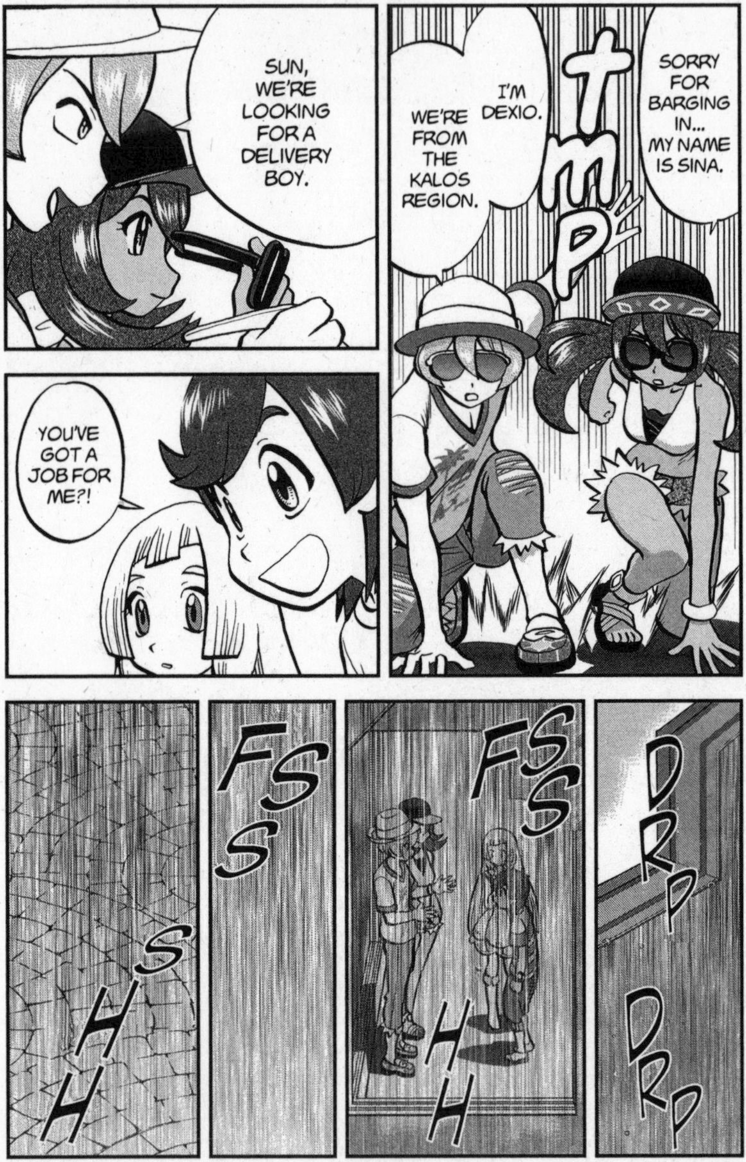
SORRY FOR BARGING IN... MY NAME IS SINA.
TMP
I'M DEXIO.
WE'RE FROM THE KALOS REGION.
SUN, WE'RE LOOKING FOR A DELIVERY BOY.
YOU'VE GOT A JOB FOR ME?!
DRP
DRP
FSS
HH
FSS
SHH

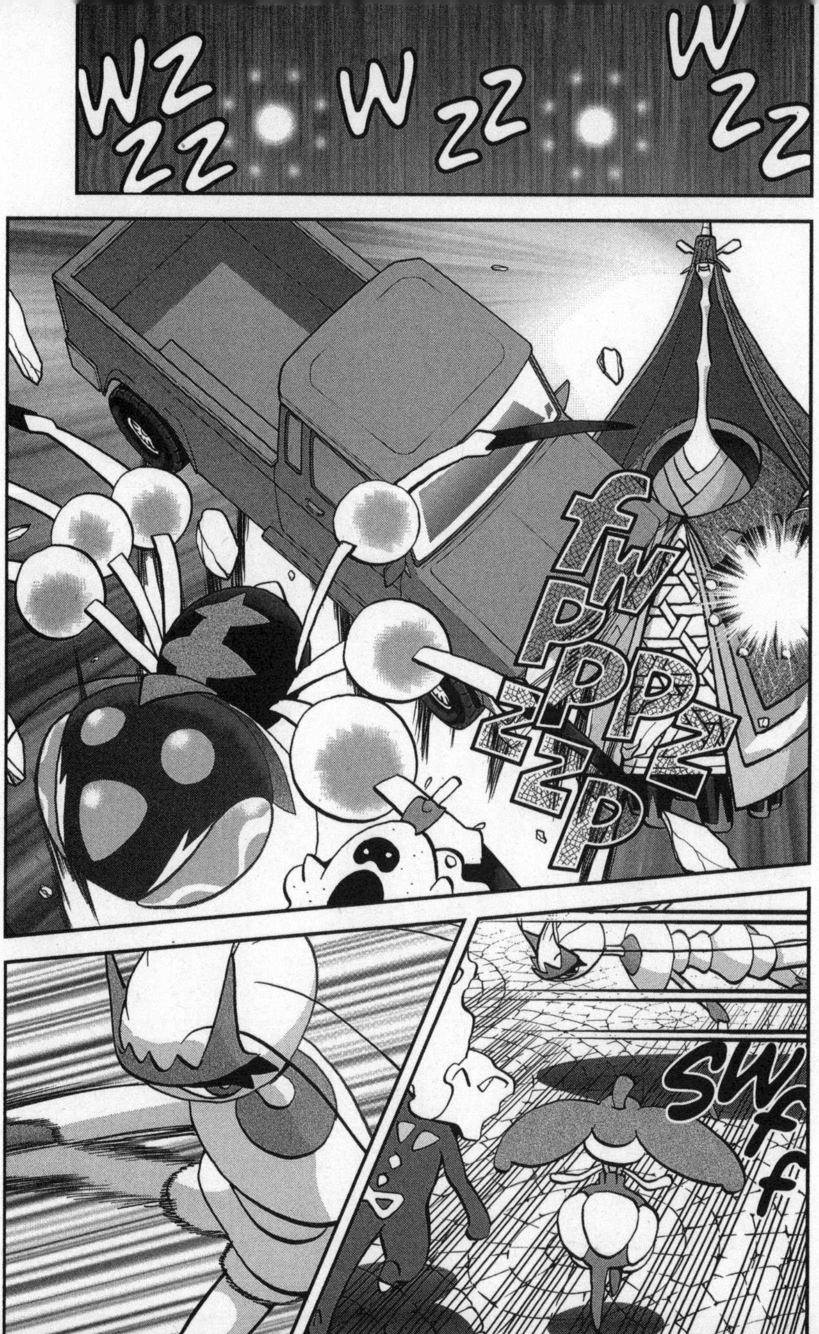
WZZZ
WZZ
WZZZ
fwPPPZZZP
SWff

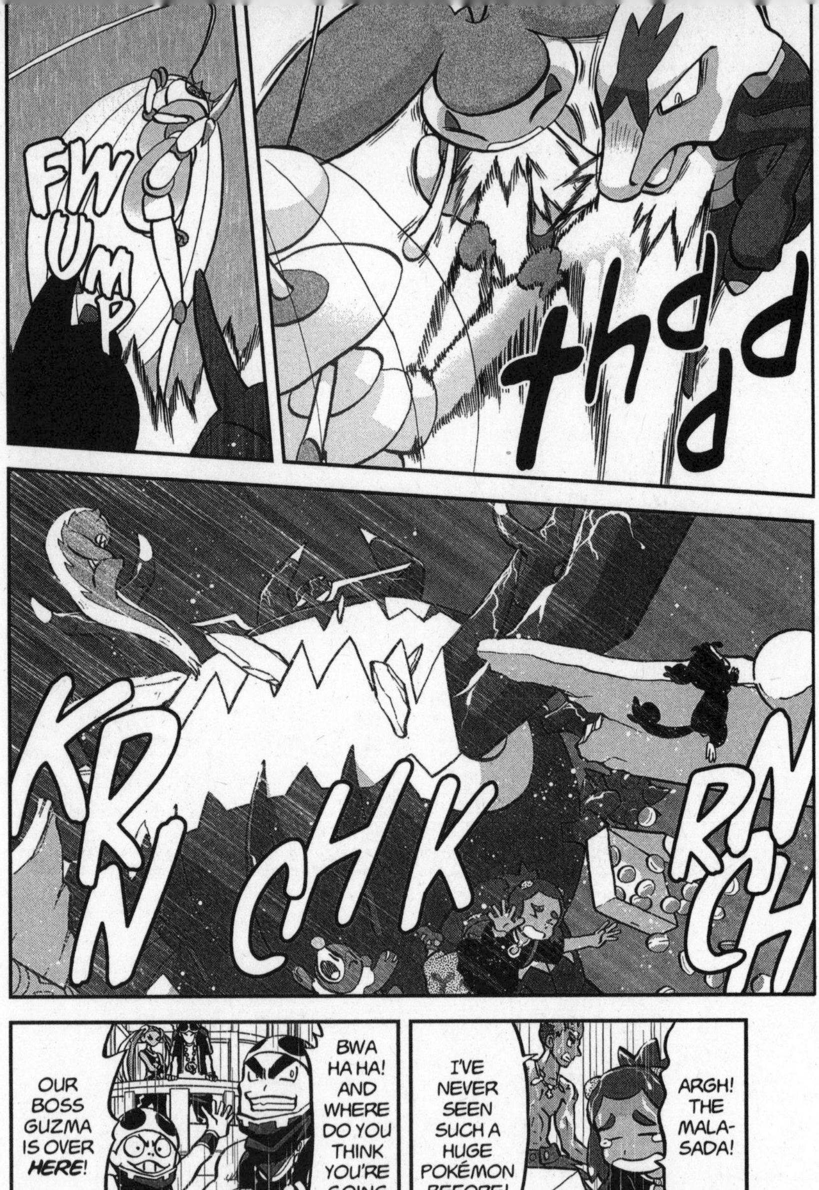
thdd
FWUMP
KRNCHK
RNCH
ARGH! THE MALASADA!
I'VE NEVER SEEN SUCH A HUGE POKÉMON BEFORE!
BWA HA HA! AND WHERE DO YOU THINK YOU'RE GOING?!
OUR BOSS GUZMA IS OVER *HERE*!

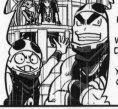

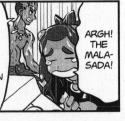

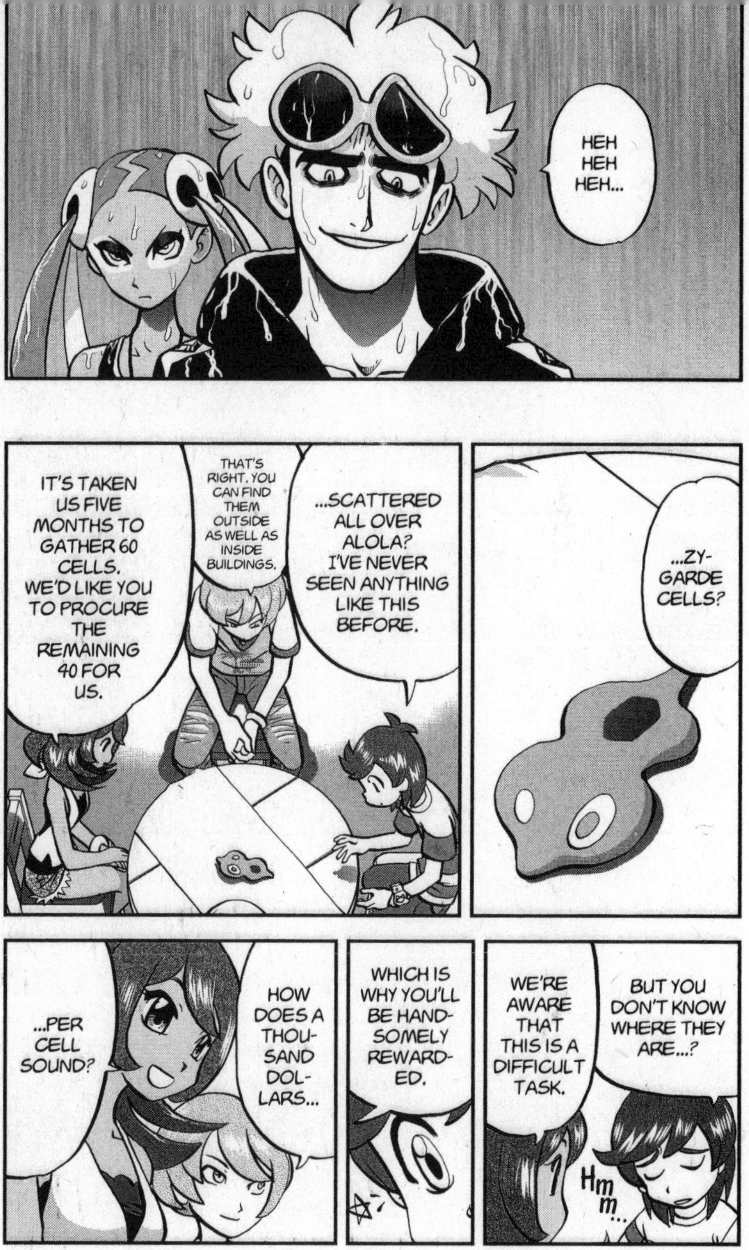
HEH HEH HEH...
...ZY-GARDE CELLS?
...SCATTERED ALL OVER ALOLA? I'VE NEVER SEEN ANYTHING LIKE THIS BEFORE.
THAT'S RIGHT. YOU CAN FIND THEM OUTSIDE AS WELL AS INSIDE BUILDINGS.
IT'S TAKEN US FIVE MONTHS TO GATHER 60 CELLS. WE'D LIKE YOU TO PROCURE THE REMAINING 40 FOR US.
BUT YOU DON'T KNOW WHERE THEY ARE...?
WE'RE AWARE THAT THIS IS A DIFFICULT TASK.
Hmm m...
WHICH IS WHY YOU'LL BE HAND-SOMELY REWARD-ED.
HOW DOES A THOU-SAND DOL-LARS...
...PER CELL SOUND?

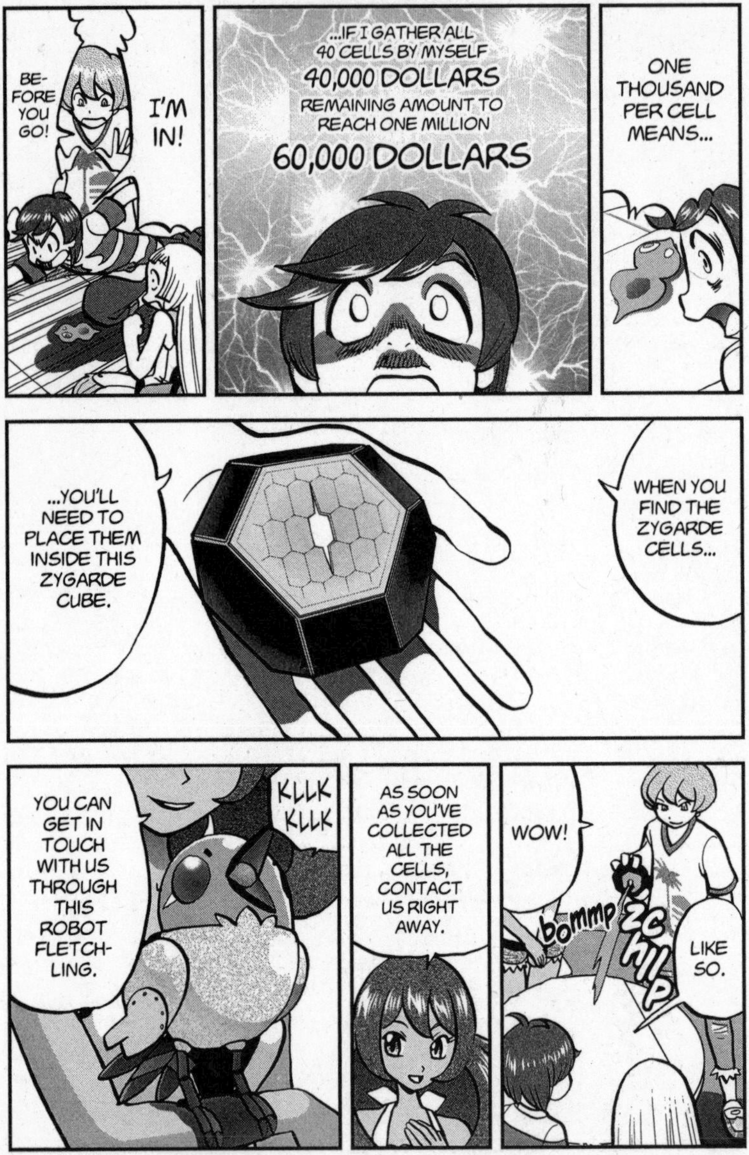
ONE THOUSAND PER CELL MEANS...
...IF I GATHER ALL 40 CELLS BY MYSELF
40,000 DOLLARS
REMAINING AMOUNT TO REACH ONE MILLION
60,000 DOLLARS
I'M IN!
BE-FORE YOU GO!
WHEN YOU FIND THE ZYGARDE CELLS...
...YOU'LL NEED TO PLACE THEM INSIDE THIS ZYGARDE CUBE.
WOW!
LIKE SO.
ZCHIP
bommp
AS SOON AS YOU'VE COLLECTED ALL THE CELLS, CONTACT US RIGHT AWAY.
KLLK KLLK
YOU CAN GET IN TOUCH WITH US THROUGH THIS ROBOT FLETCH-LING.

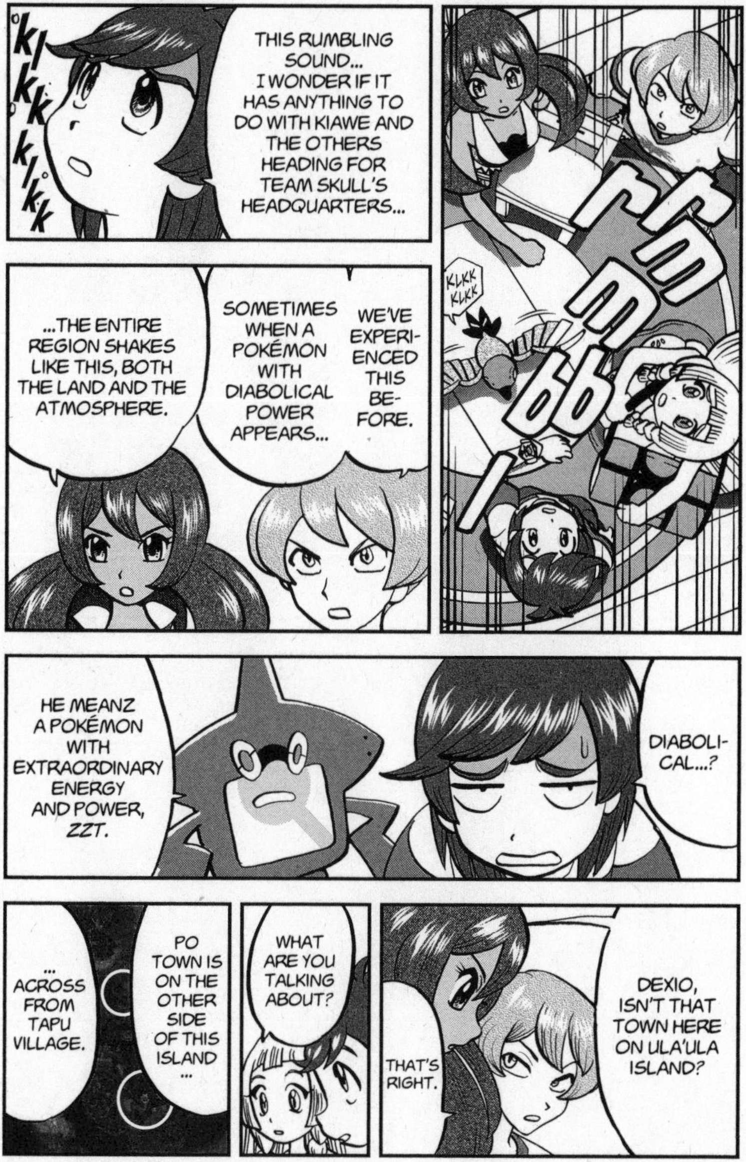
KLKK KLKK
THIS RUMBLING SOUND... I WONDER IF IT HAS ANYTHING TO DO WITH KIAWE AND THE OTHERS HEADING FOR TEAM SKULL'S HEADQUARTERS...
WE'VE EXPERIENCED THIS BEFORE.
SOMETIMES WHEN A POKÉMON WITH DIABOLICAL POWER APPEARS...
...THE ENTIRE REGION SHAKES LIKE THIS, BOTH THE LAND AND THE ATMOSPHERE.
DIABOLICAL...?
HE MEANZ A POKÉMON WITH EXTRAORDINARY ENERGY AND POWER, ZZT.
DEXIO, ISN'T THAT TOWN HERE ON ULA'ULA ISLAND?
THAT'S RIGHT.
WHAT ARE YOU TALKING ABOUT?
PO TOWN IS ON THE OTHER SIDE OF THIS ISLAND...
...ACROSS FROM TAPU VILLAGE.

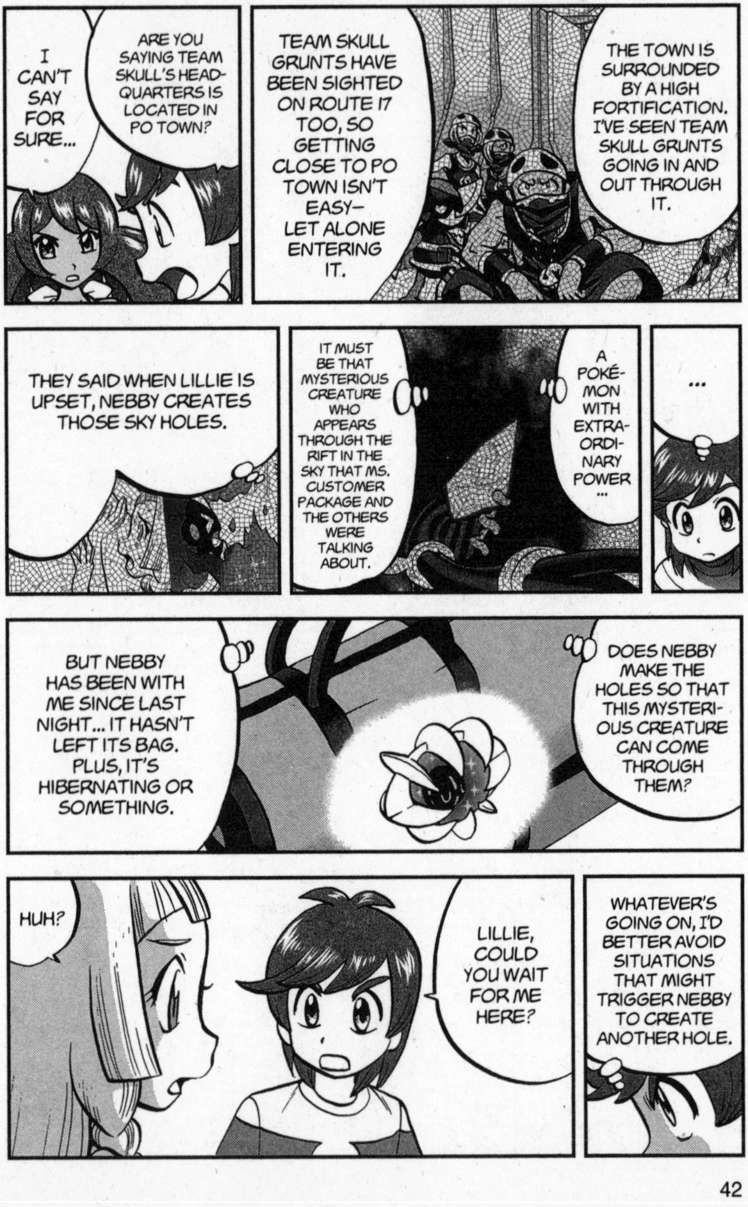
THE TOWN IS SURROUNDED BY A HIGH FORTIFICATION. I'VE SEEN TEAM SKULL GRUNTS GOING IN AND OUT THROUGH IT.
TEAM SKULL GRUNTS HAVE BEEN SIGHTED ON ROUTE 17 TOO, SO GETTING CLOSE TO PO TOWN ISN'T EASY— LET ALONE ENTERING IT.
ARE YOU SAYING TEAM SKULL'S HEAD-QUARTERS IS LOCATED IN PO TOWN?
I CAN'T SAY FOR SURE...
...
A POKÉ-MON WITH EXTRA-ORDI-NARY POWER ...
IT MUST BE THAT MYSTERIOUS CREATURE WHO APPEARS THROUGH THE RIFT IN THE SKY THAT MS. CUSTOMER PACKAGE AND THE OTHERS WERE TALKING ABOUT.
THEY SAID WHEN LILLIE IS UPSET, NEBBY CREATES THOSE SKY HOLES.
DOES NEBBY MAKE THE HOLES SO THAT THIS MYSTERI-OUS CREATURE CAN COME THROUGH THEM?
BUT NEBBY HAS BEEN WITH ME SINCE LAST NIGHT... IT HASN'T LEFT ITS BAG. PLUS, IT'S HIBERNATING OR SOMETHING.
WHATEVER'S GOING ON, I'D BETTER AVOID SITUATIONS THAT MIGHT TRIGGER NEBBY TO CREATE ANOTHER HOLE.
LILLIE, COULD YOU WAIT FOR ME HERE?
HUH?

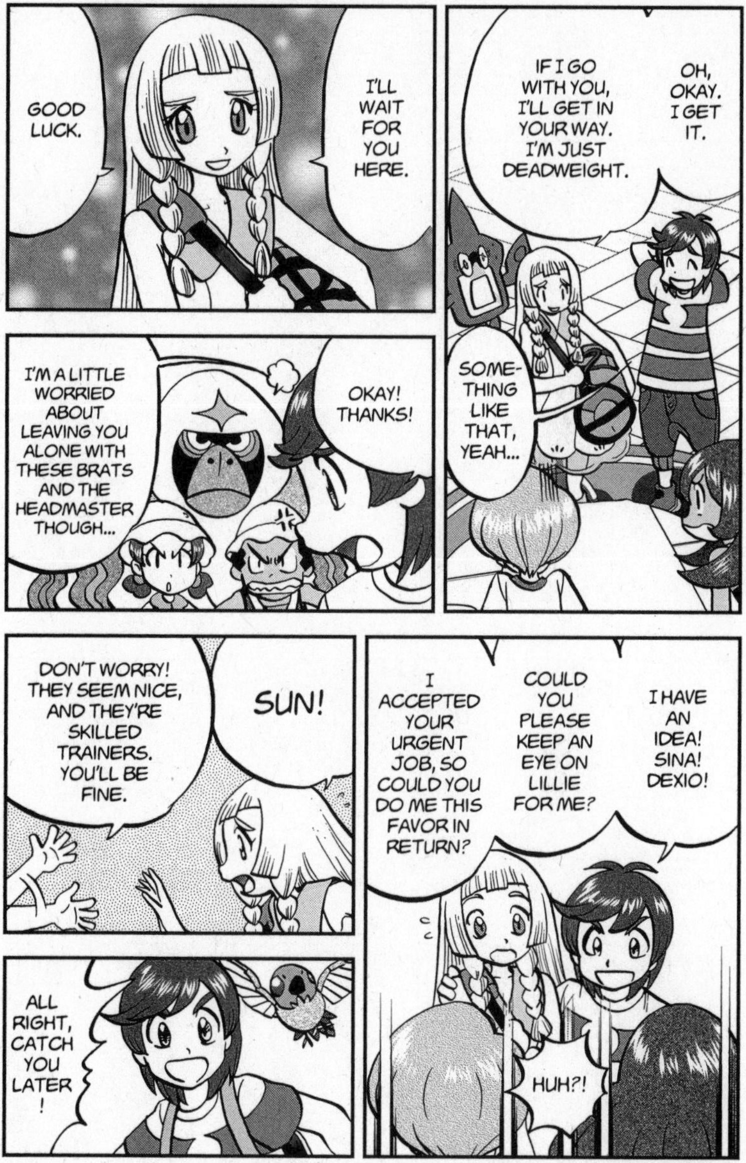
OH, OKAY. I GET IT.
IF I GO WITH YOU, I'LL GET IN YOUR WAY. I'M JUST DEADWEIGHT.
SOME-THING LIKE THAT, YEAH...
I'LL WAIT FOR YOU HERE.
GOOD LUCK.
OKAY! THANKS!
I'M A LITTLE WORRIED ABOUT LEAVING YOU ALONE WITH THESE BRATS AND THE HEADMASTER THOUGH...
I HAVE AN IDEA! SINA! DEXIO!
COULD YOU PLEASE KEEP AN EYE ON LILLIE FOR ME?
I ACCEPTED YOUR URGENT JOB, SO COULD YOU DO ME THIS FAVOR IN RETURN?
HUH?!
SUN!
DON'T WORRY! THEY SEEM NICE, AND THEY'RE SKILLED TRAINERS. YOU'LL BE FINE.
ALL RIGHT, CATCH YOU LATER!

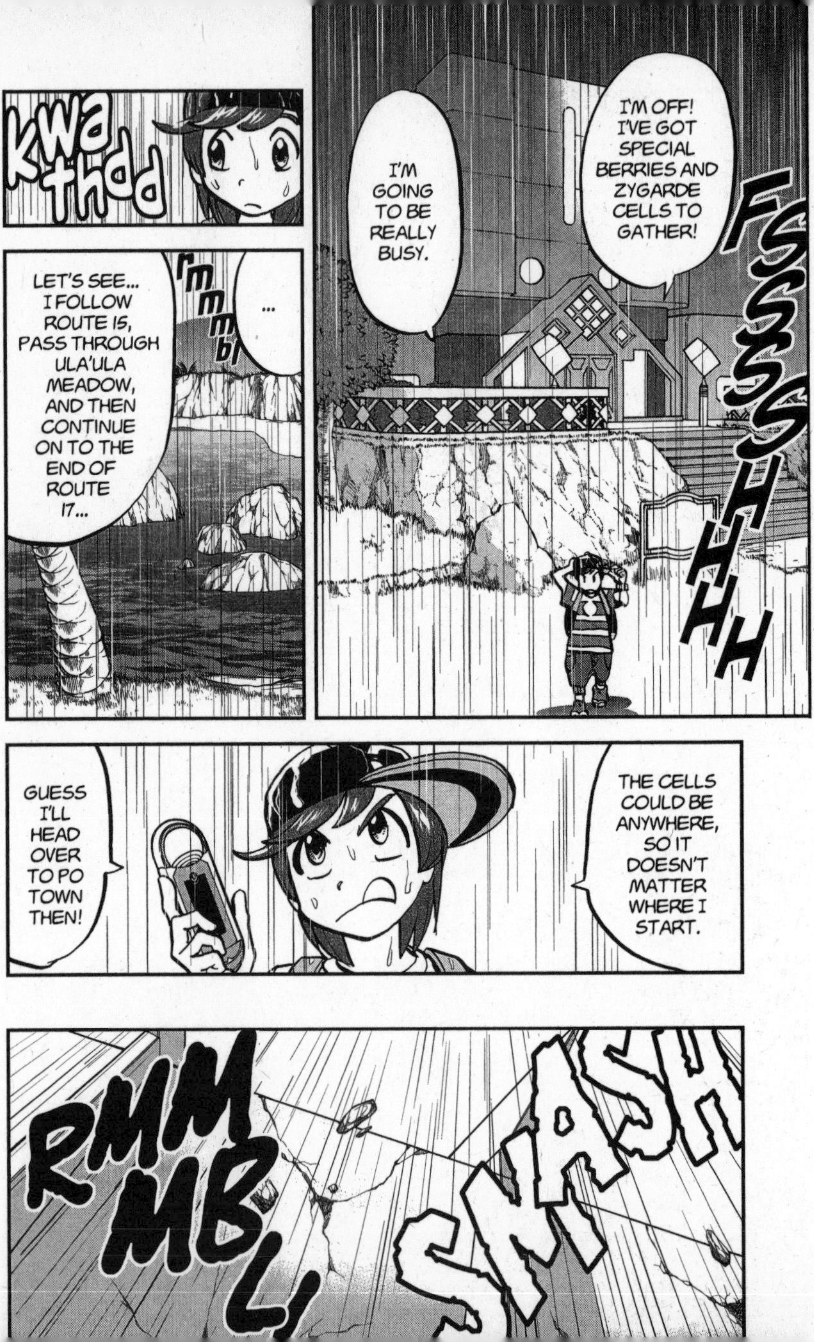
I'M OFF! I'VE GOT SPECIAL BERRIES AND ZYGARDE CELLS TO GATHER!
I'M GOING TO BE REALLY BUSY.
FSSSSHHHHH
kwa thdd
...
rmmmbl
LET'S SEE... I FOLLOW ROUTE 15, PASS THROUGH ULA'ULA MEADOW, AND THEN CONTINUE ON TO THE END OF ROUTE 17...
THE CELLS COULD BE ANYWHERE, SO IT DOESN'T MATTER WHERE I START.
GUESS I'LL HEAD OVER TO PO TOWN THEN!
SKASH
RMMMBL

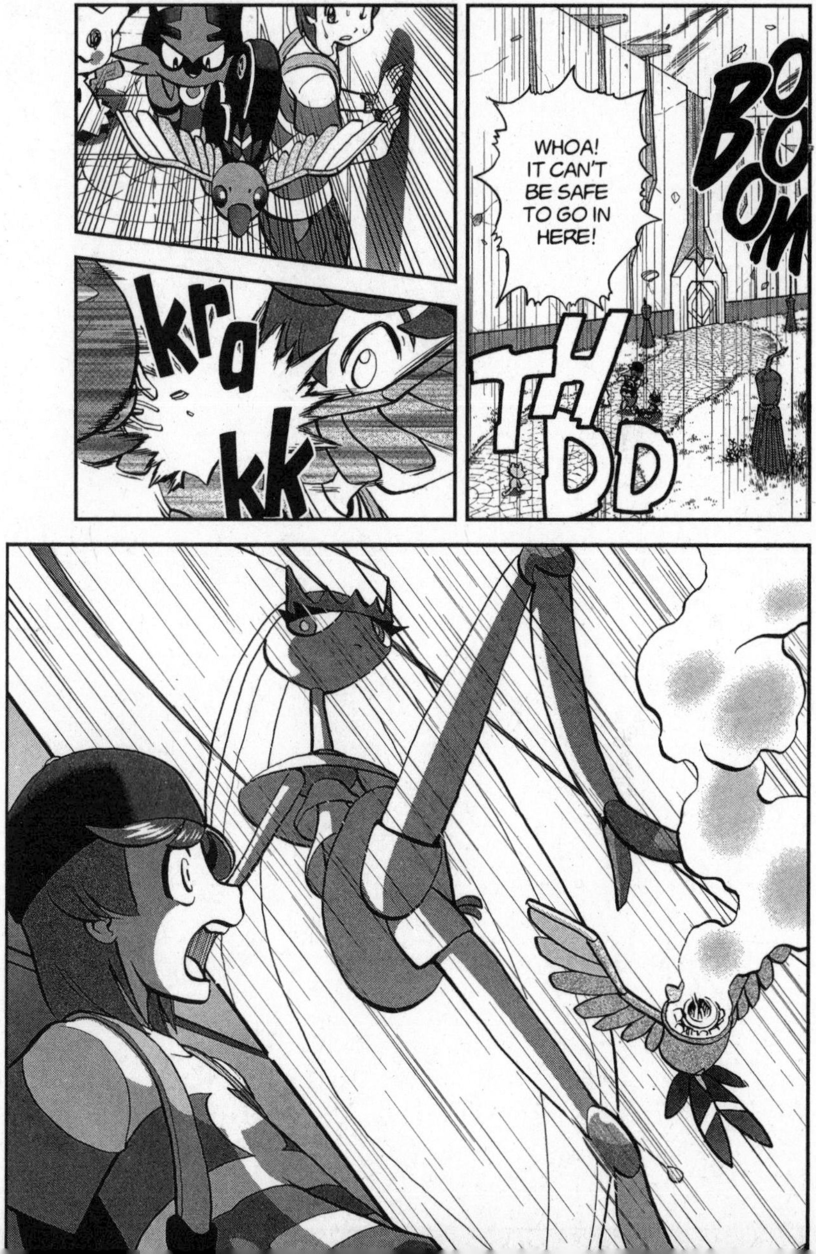
BOOOM
WHOA! IT CAN'T BE SAFE TO GO IN HERE!
THDD
krakk

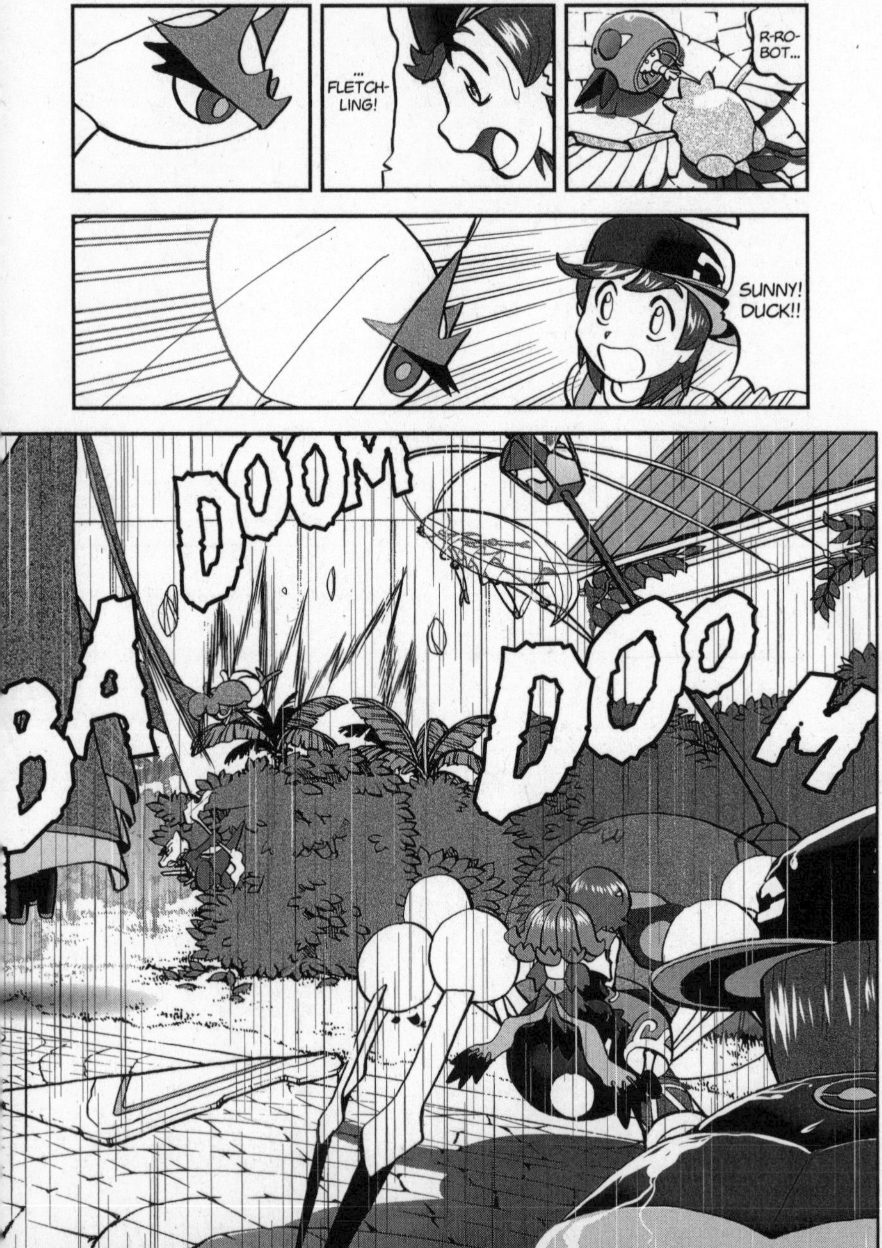
R-RO-BOT...
... FLETCH-LING!
SUNNY! DUCK!!
DOOM
DOOM
BA

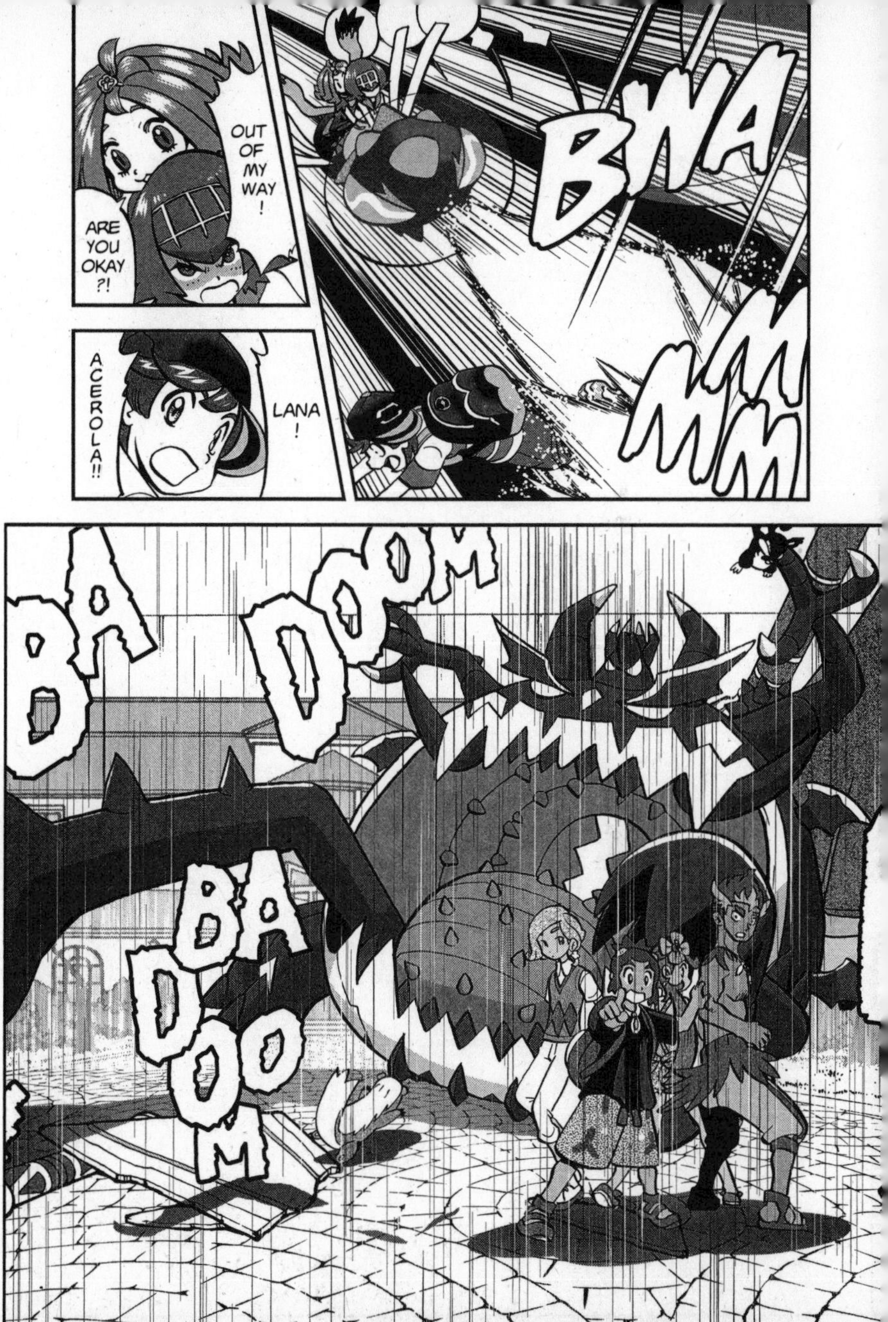
BWAMMM
OUT OF MY WAY!
ARE YOU OKAY?!
LANA!
ACEROLA!!
BA DOOM
BA DOOM

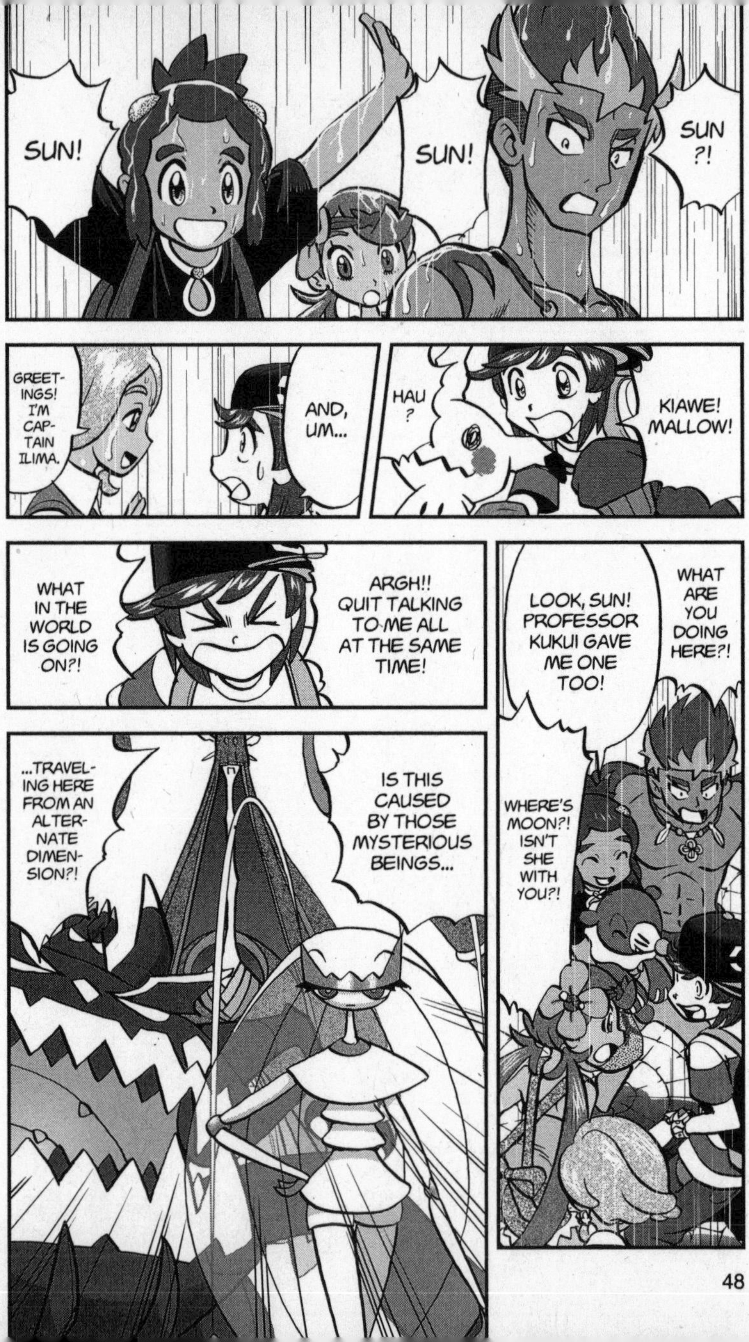
SUN ?!
SUN!
SUN!
KIAWE! MALLOW!
HAU ?
AND, UM...
GREETINGS! I'M CAPTAIN ILIMA.
WHAT ARE YOU DOING HERE?!
LOOK, SUN! PROFESSOR KUKUI GAVE ME ONE TOO!
WHERE'S MOON?! ISN'T SHE WITH YOU?!
ARGH!! QUIT TALKING TO ME ALL AT THE SAME TIME!
WHAT IN THE WORLD IS GOING ON?!
IS THIS CAUSED BY THOSE MYSTERIOUS BEINGS...
...TRAVELING HERE FROM AN ALTERNATE DIMENSION?!

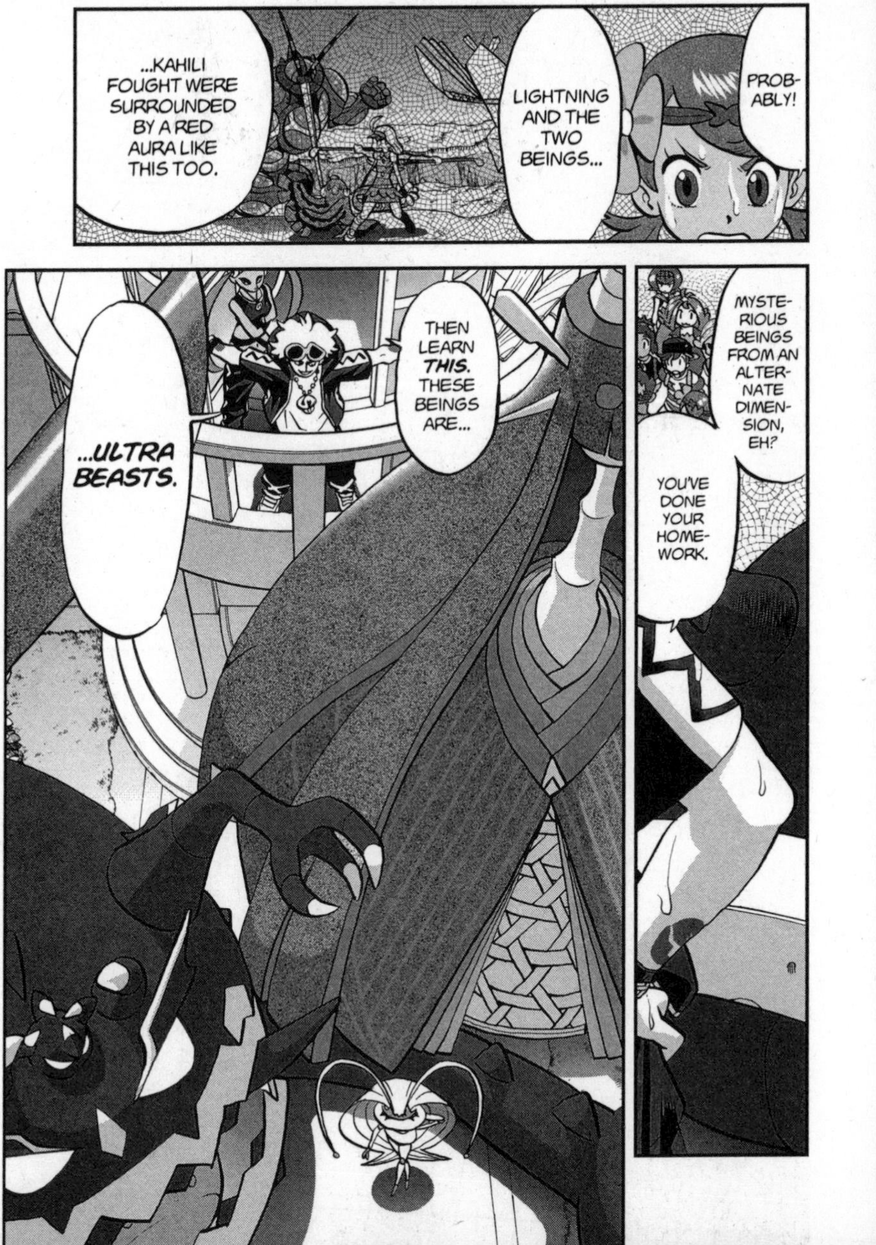
PROB-ABLY!
LIGHTNING AND THE TWO BEINGS...
...KAHILI FOUGHT WERE SURROUNDED BY A RED AURA LIKE THIS TOO.
MYSTE-RIOUS BEINGS FROM AN ALTER-NATE DIMEN-SION, EH?
YOU'VE DONE YOUR HOME-WORK.
THEN LEARN *THIS*. THESE BEINGS ARE...
...ULTRA BEASTS.

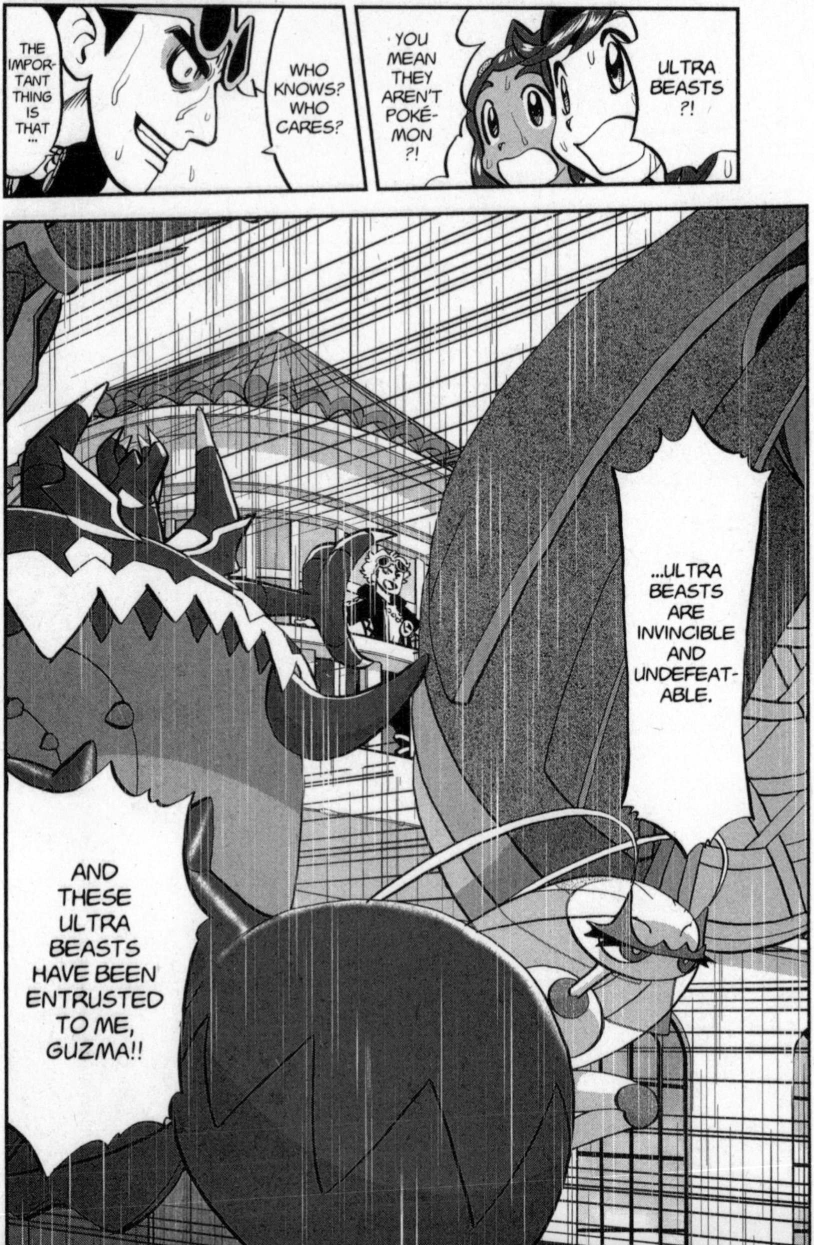
ULTRA BEASTS?!
YOU MEAN THEY AREN'T POKÉMON?!
WHO KNOWS? WHO CARES?
THE IMPORTANT THING IS THAT...
...ULTRA BEASTS ARE INVINCIBLE AND UNDEFEATABLE.
AND THESE ULTRA BEASTS HAVE BEEN ENTRUSTED TO ME, GUZMA!!

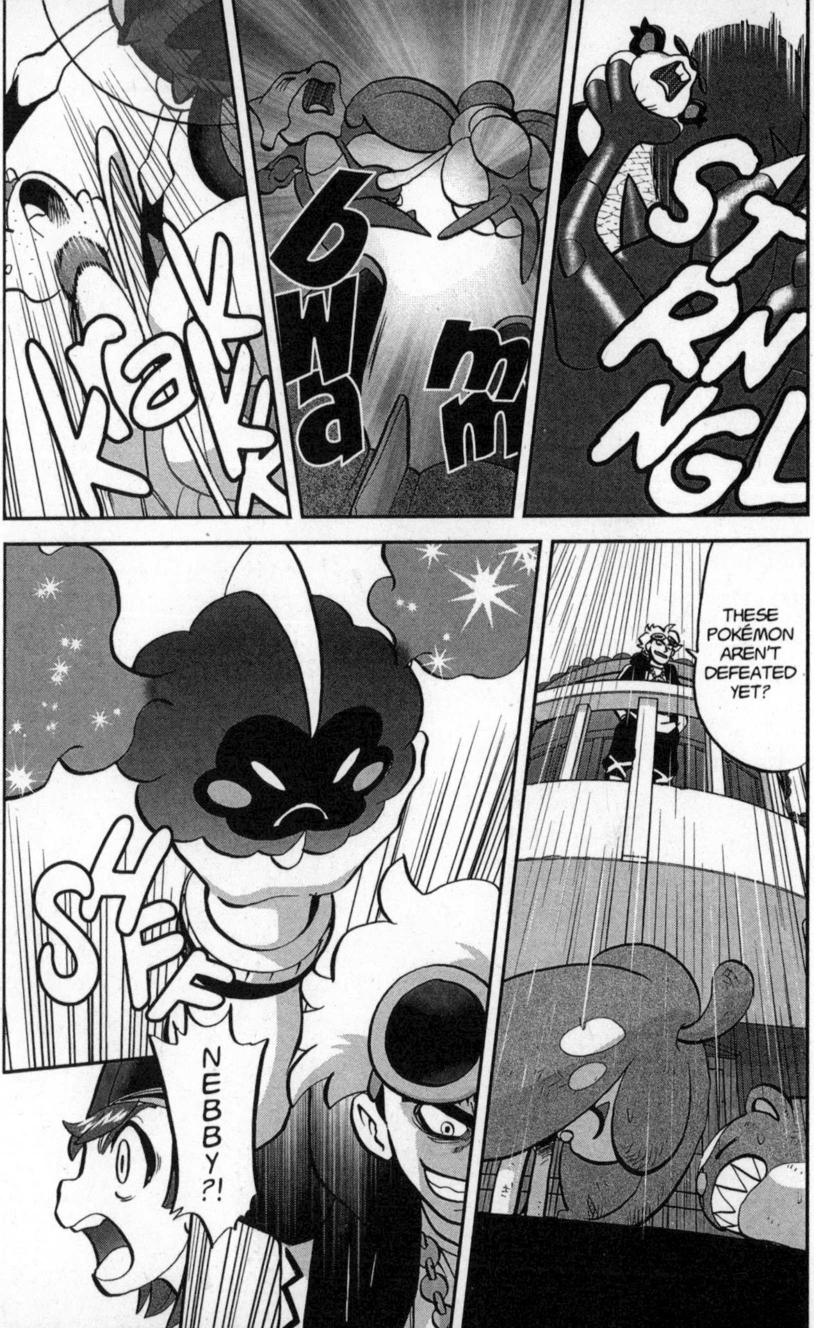
ST
RN
NGL
bwamm
krakk
THESE POKÉMON AREN'T DEFEATED YET?
SHF
NEBBY?!

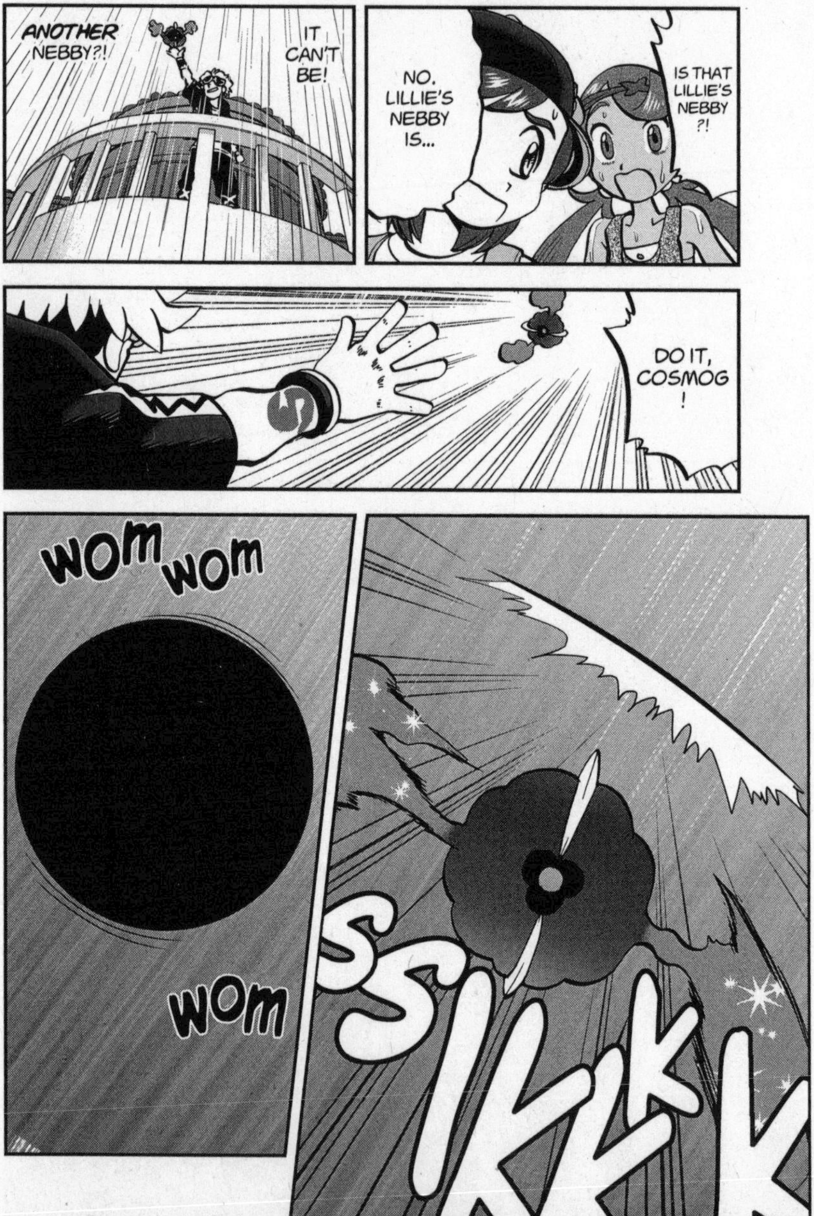
IS THAT LILLIE'S NEBBY?!
NO. LILLIE'S NEBBY IS...
IT CAN'T BE!
ANOTHER NEBBY?!
DO IT, COSMOG!
SSIKKKK
wom wom
wom

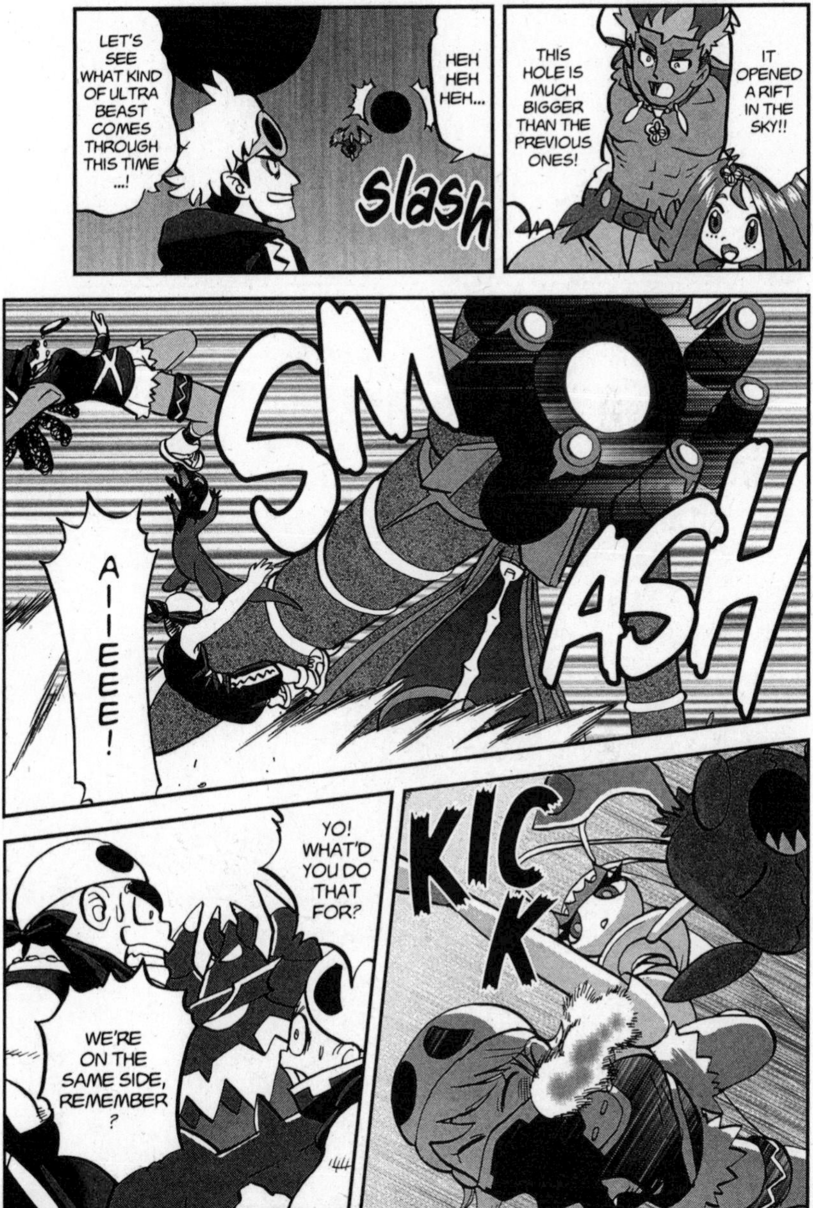
IT OPENED A RIFT IN THE SKY!!
THIS HOLE IS MUCH BIGGER THAN THE PREVIOUS ONES!
HEH HEH HEH...
LET'S SEE WHAT KIND OF ULTRA BEAST COMES THROUGH THIS TIME ...!
slash
SMASH
AIIEEE!
KICK
YO! WHAT'D YOU DO THAT FOR?
WE'RE ON THE SAME SIDE, REMEMBER ?

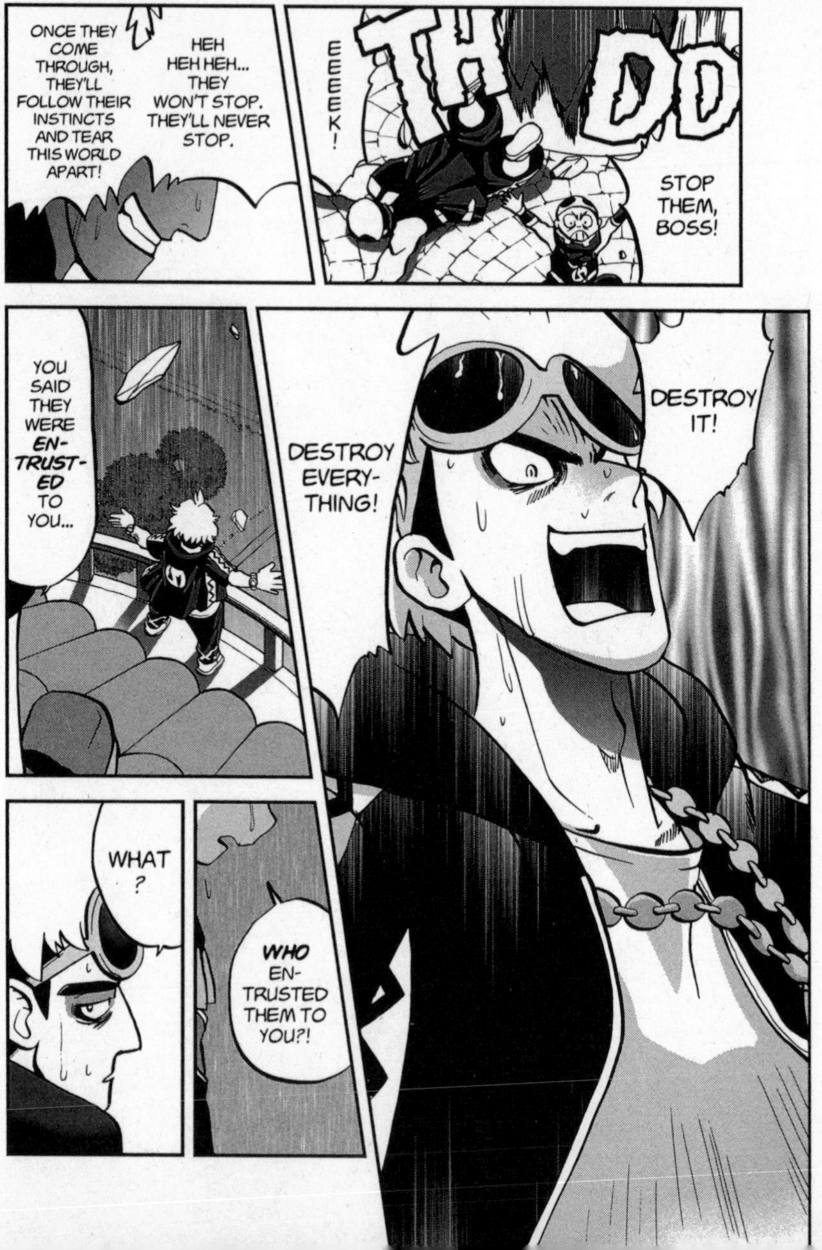
THWDD
EEEEEK!
STOP THEM, BOSS!
HEH HEH HEH... THEY WON'T STOP. THEY'LL NEVER STOP.
ONCE THEY COME THROUGH, THEY'LL FOLLOW THEIR INSTINCTS AND TEAR THIS WORLD APART!
DESTROY IT!
DESTROY EVERYTHING!
YOU SAID THEY WERE *ENTRUSTED* TO YOU...
WHO ENTRUSTED THEM TO YOU?!
WHAT?

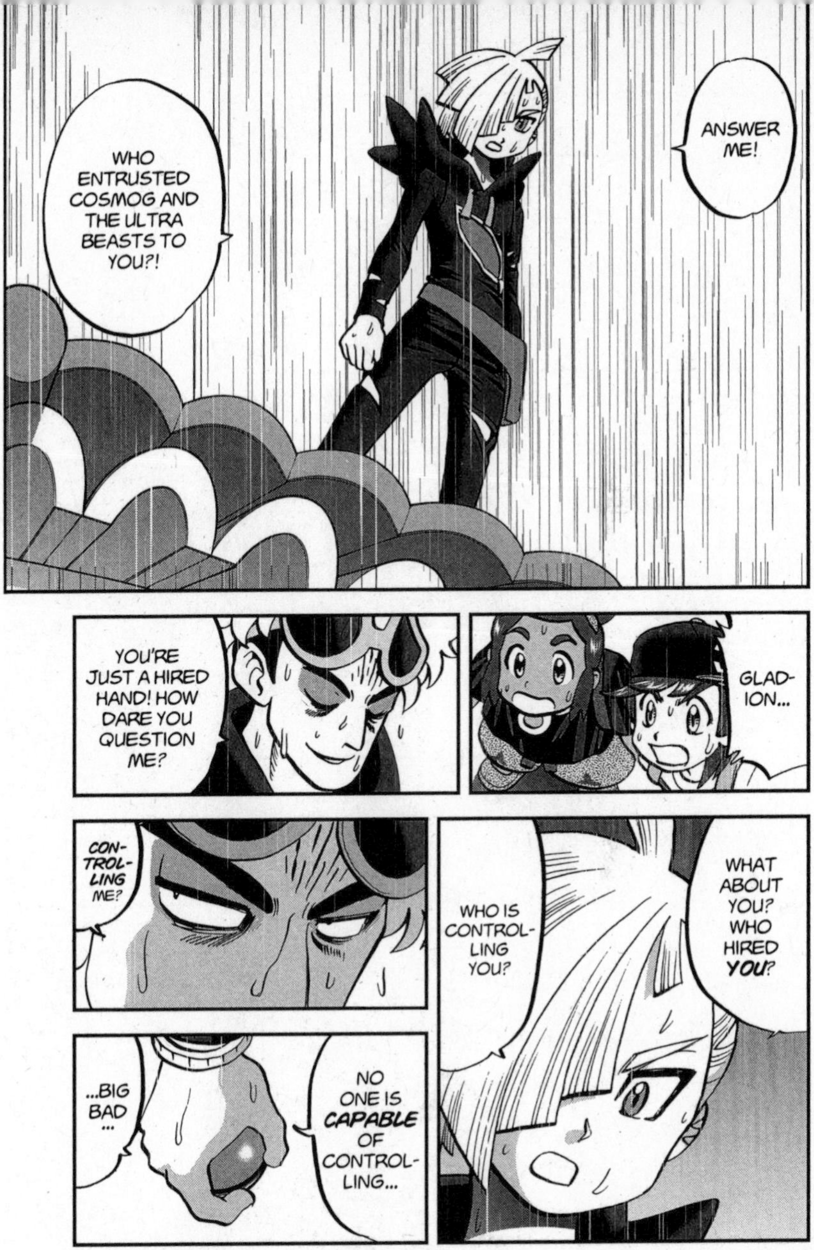
ANSWER ME!
WHO ENTRUSTED COSMOG AND THE ULTRA BEASTS TO YOU?!
GLAD-ION...
YOU'RE JUST A HIRED HAND! HOW DARE YOU QUESTION ME?
WHAT ABOUT YOU? WHO HIRED ***YOU***?
WHO IS CONTROL-LING YOU?
CON-TROL-LING ME?
NO ONE IS ***CAPABLE*** OF CONTROL-LING...
...BIG BAD ...

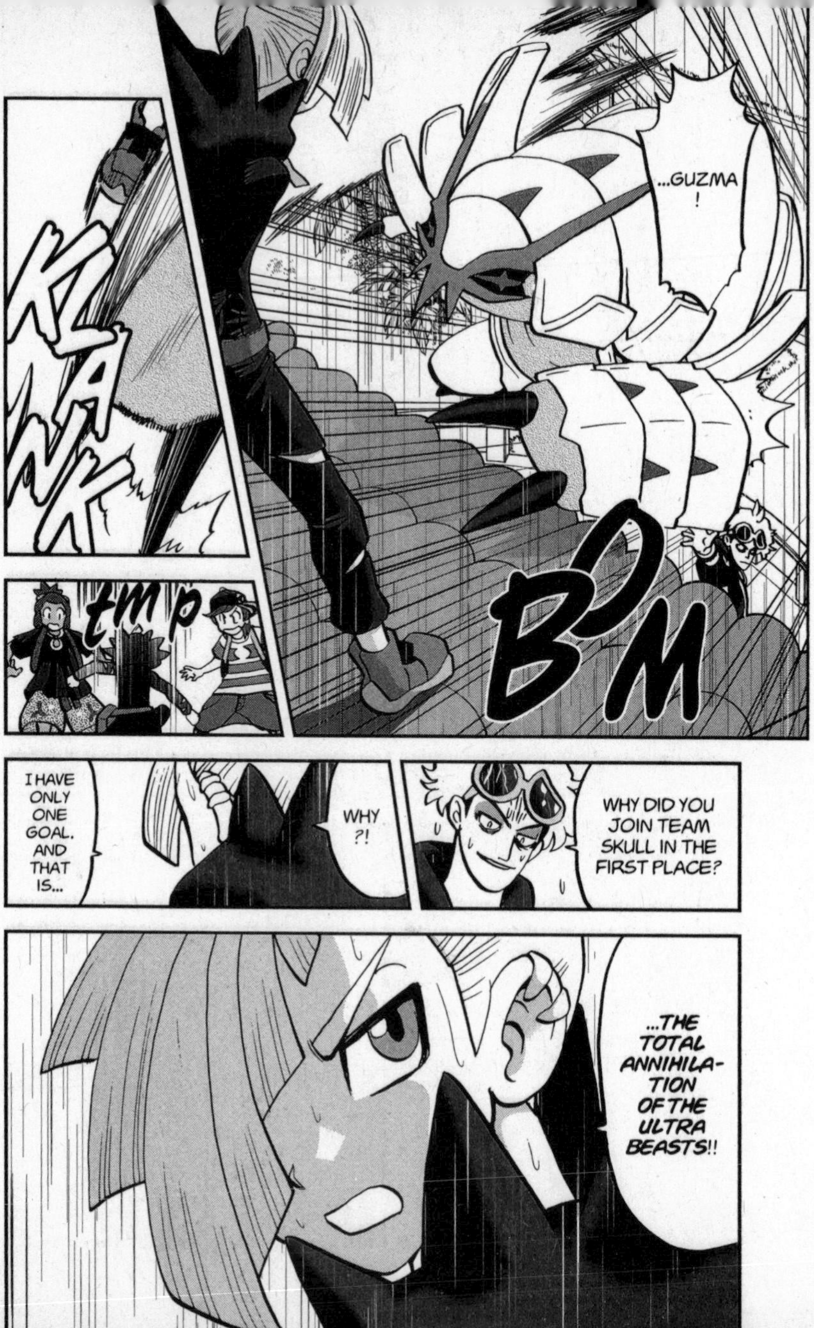
...GUZMA !
BOOM
KLANK
tmp
WHY DID YOU JOIN TEAM SKULL IN THE FIRST PLACE?
WHY ?!
I HAVE ONLY ONE GOAL. AND THAT IS...
...THE TOTAL ANNIHILATION OF THE ULTRA BEASTS!!

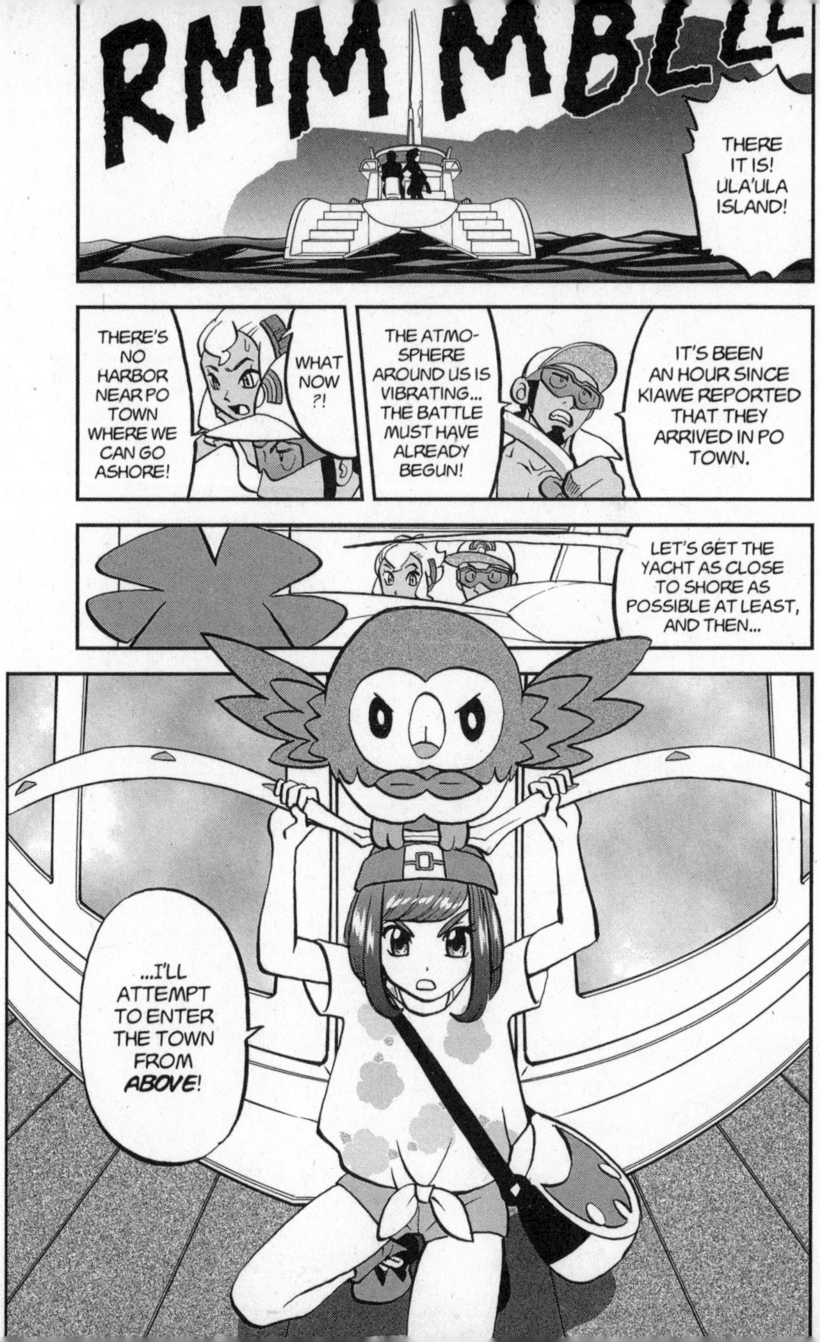
RMMMBLLL
THERE IT IS! ULA'ULA ISLAND!
IT'S BEEN AN HOUR SINCE KIAWE REPORTED THAT THEY ARRIVED IN PO TOWN.
THE ATMOSPHERE AROUND US IS VIBRATING... THE BATTLE MUST HAVE ALREADY BEGUN!
WHAT NOW?!
THERE'S NO HARBOR NEAR PO TOWN WHERE WE CAN GO ASHORE!
LET'S GET THE YACHT AS CLOSE TO SHORE AS POSSIBLE AT LEAST, AND THEN...
...I'LL ATTEMPT TO ENTER THE TOWN FROM ABOVE!

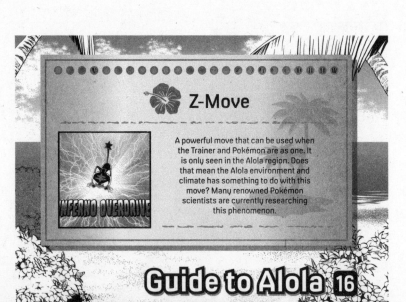

Z-Move
INFERNO OVERDRIVE
A powerful move that can be used when the Trainer and Pokémon are as one. It is only seen in the Alola region. Does that mean the Alola environment and climate has something to do with this move? Many renowned Pokémon scientists are currently researching this phenomenon.
Guide to Alola 16

Adventure 19 Truth and the Mastermind Behind Team Skull

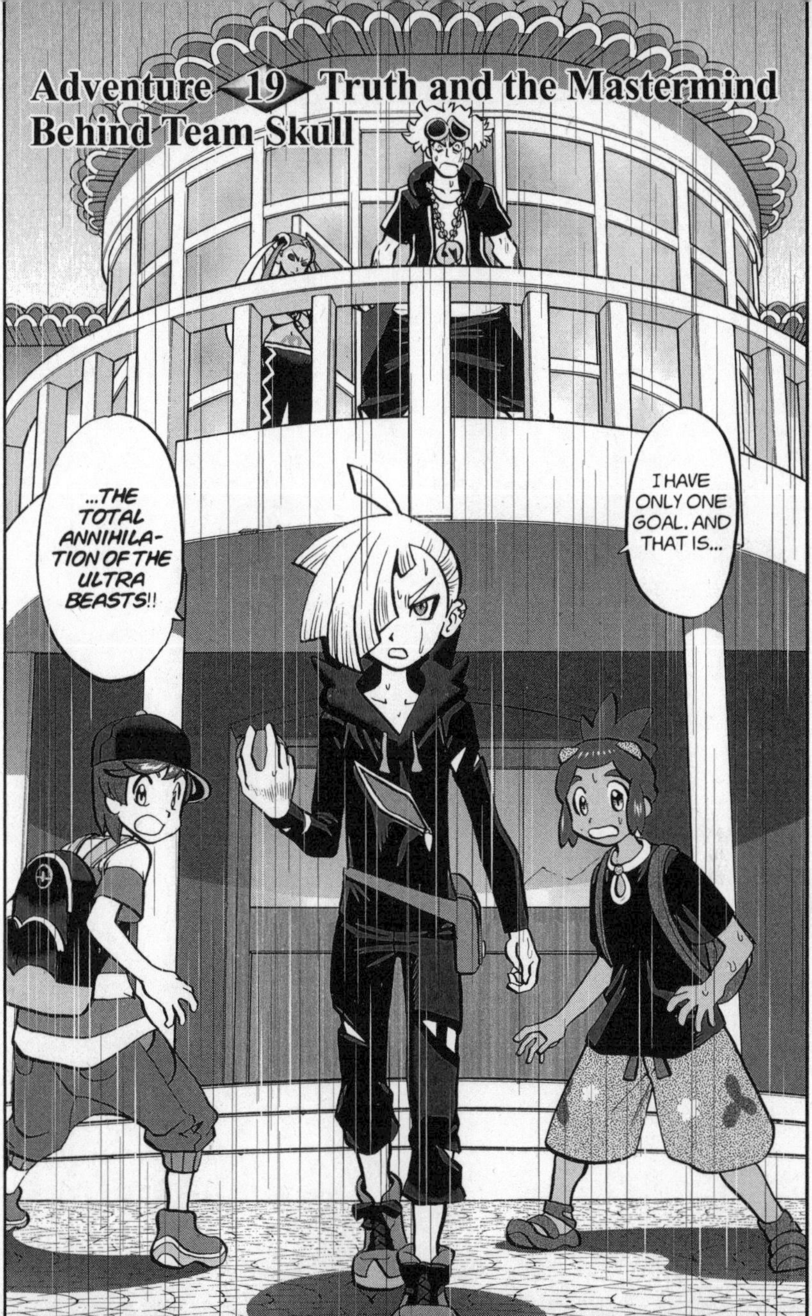
I HAVE ONLY ONE GOAL. AND THAT IS...
...THE TOTAL ANNIHILA-TION OF THE ULTRA BEASTS!!

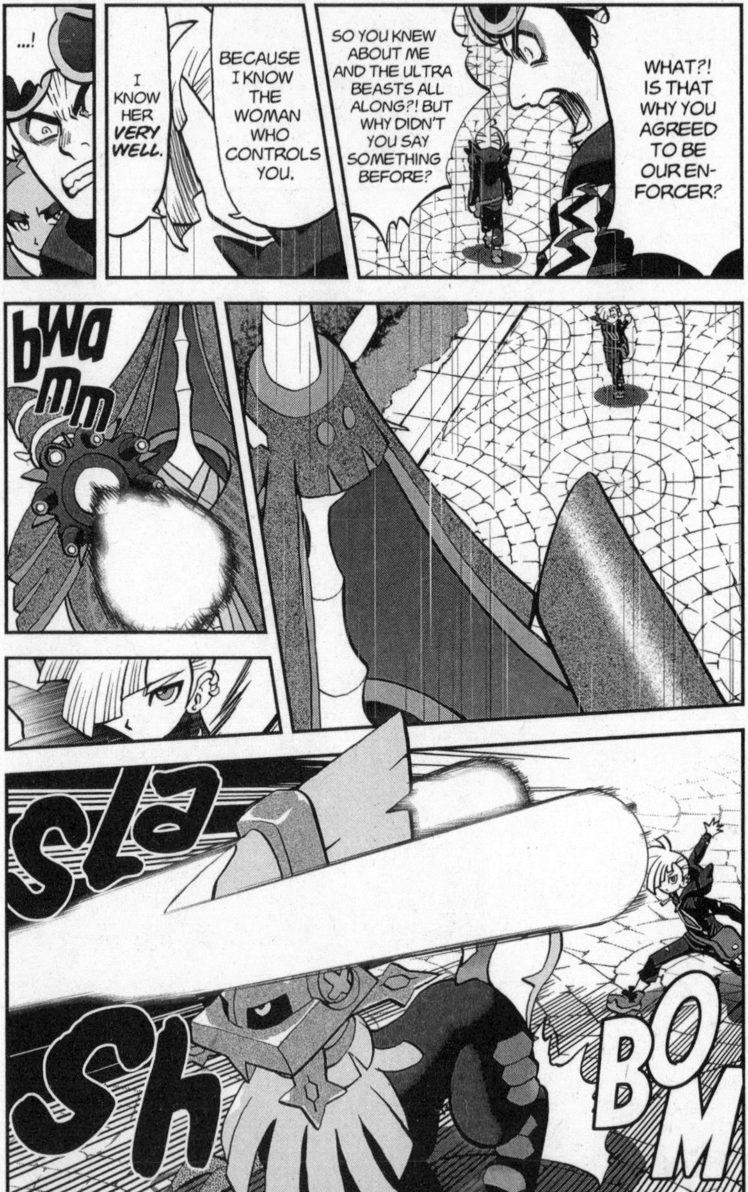
WHAT?! IS THAT WHY YOU AGREED TO BE OUR EN-FORCER?
SO YOU KNEW ABOUT ME AND THE ULTRA BEASTS ALL ALONG?! BUT WHY DIDN'T YOU SAY SOMETHING BEFORE?
BECAUSE I KNOW THE WOMAN WHO CONTROLS YOU.
I KNOW HER *VERY WELL*.
...!
bwamm
BOOM
slash

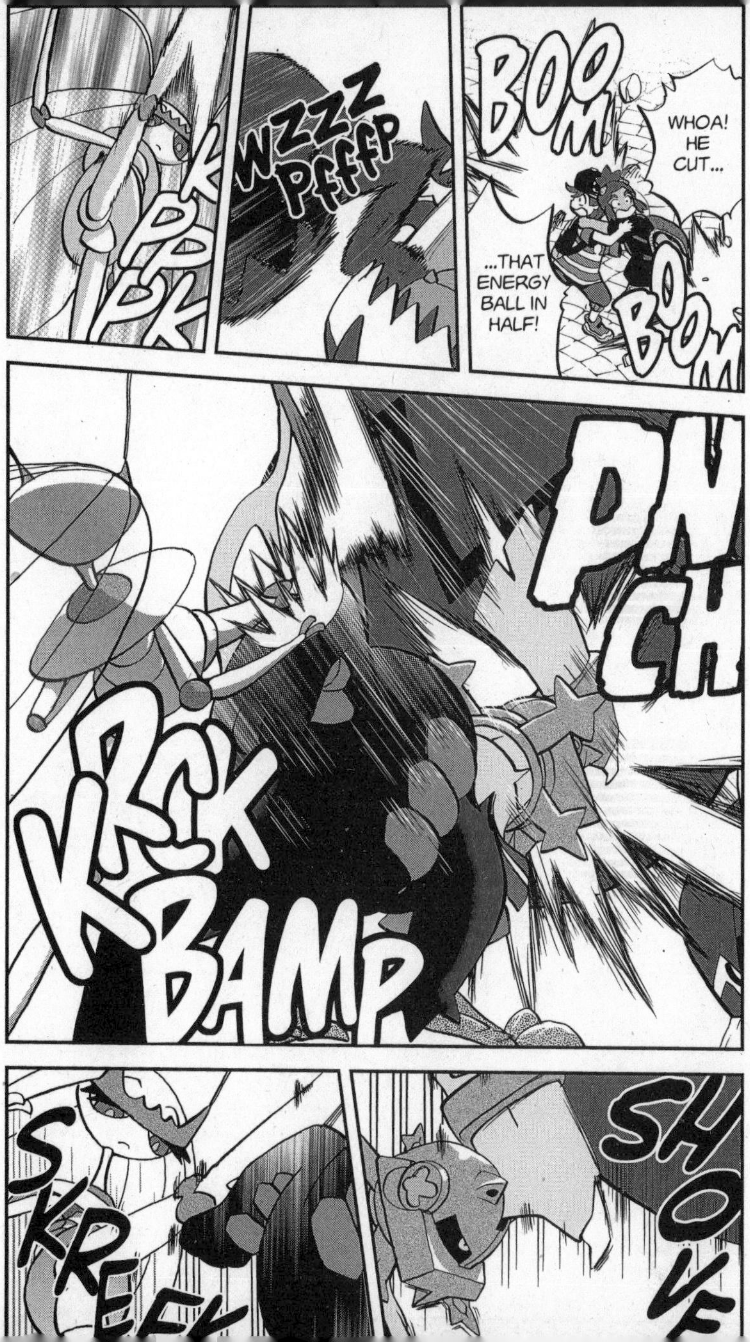
BOOM
WHOA! HE CUT...
...THAT ENERGY BALL IN HALF!
BOOM
WZZZ PFFFP
KPPPK
DN
CH
KRCK
BAMP
SHOVE
SKREE

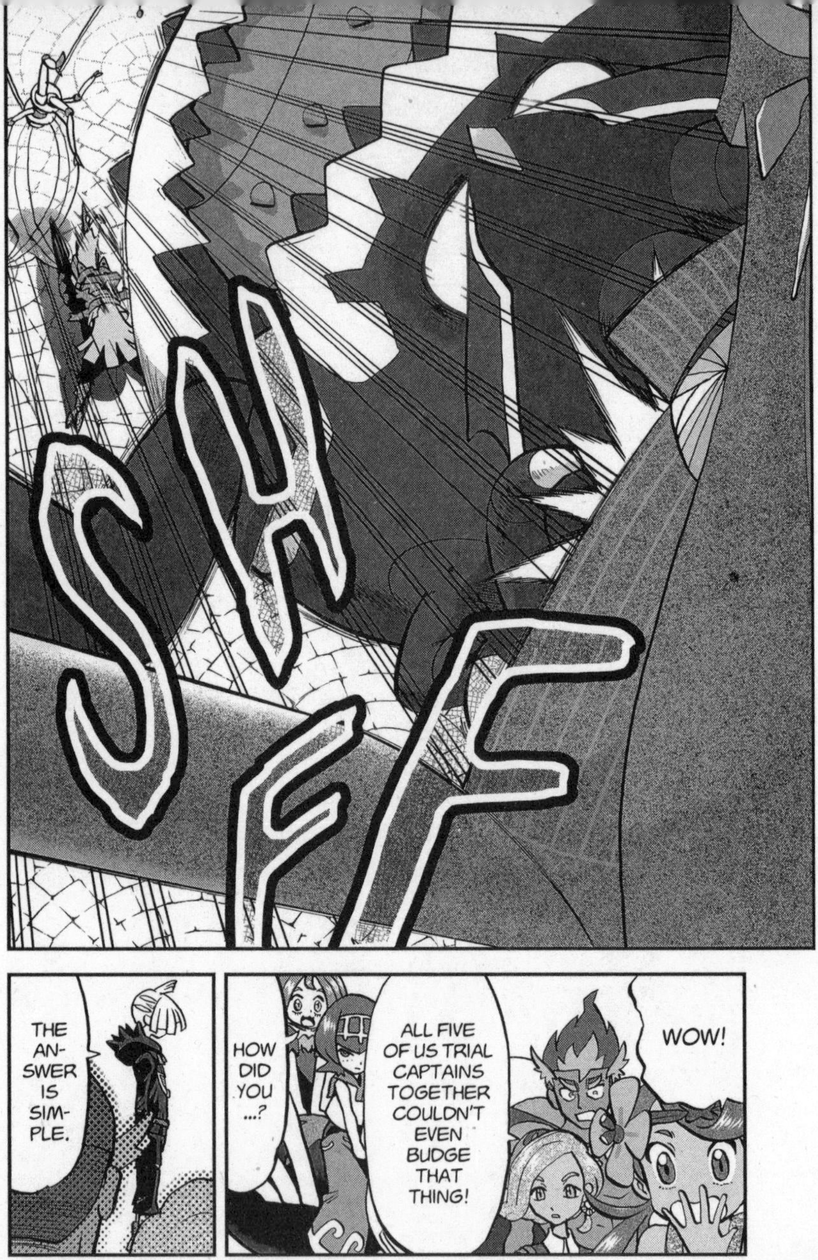
SHFF
WOW!
ALL FIVE OF US TRIAL CAPTAINS TOGETHER COULDN'T EVEN BUDGE THAT THING!
HOW DID YOU ...?
THE AN-SWER IS SIM-PLE.

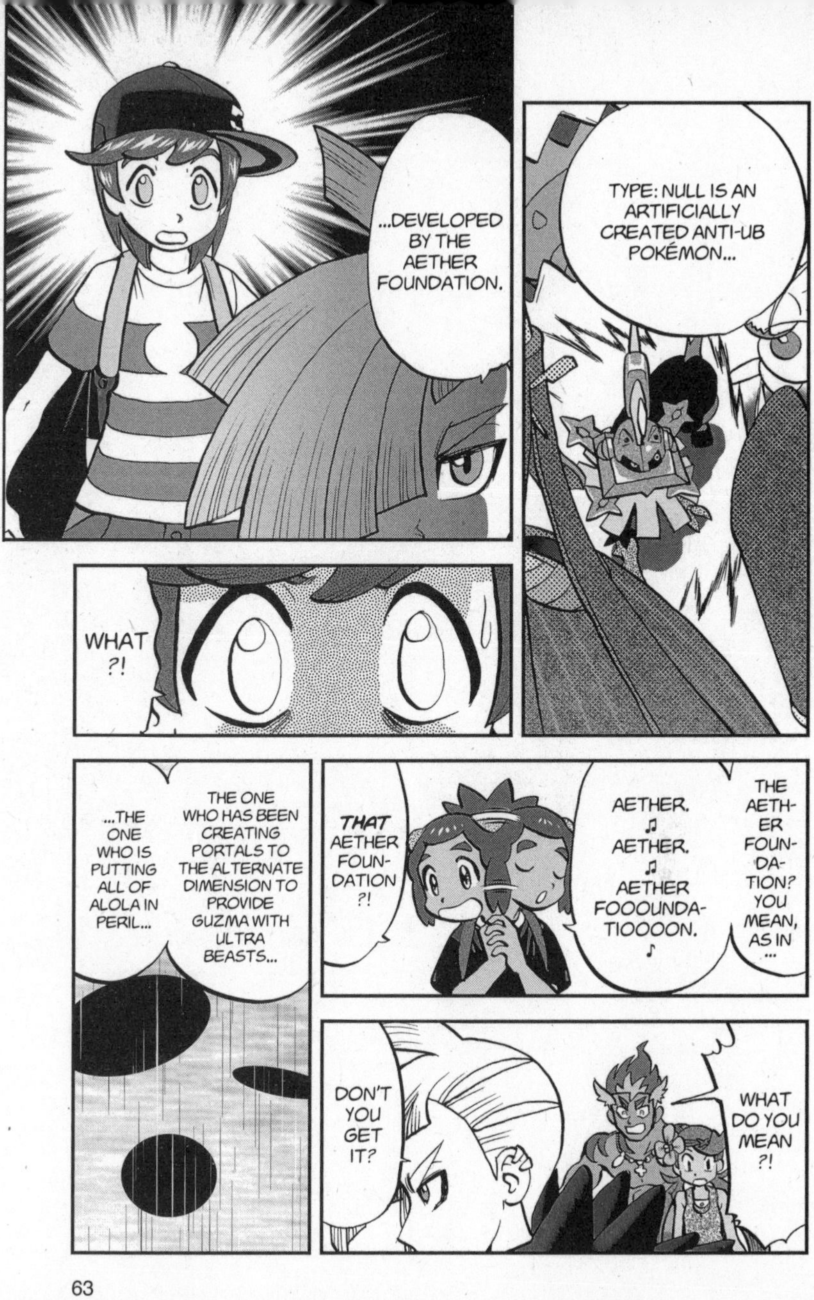
TYPE: NULL IS AN ARTIFICIALLY CREATED ANTI-UB POKÉMON...
...DEVELOPED BY THE AETHER FOUNDATION.
WHAT ?!
THE AETHER FOUNDATION? YOU MEAN, AS IN ...
AETHER. ♪ AETHER. ♪ AETHER FOOOUNDATIOOOOON. ♪
THAT AETHER FOUNDATION ?!
WHAT DO YOU MEAN ?!
DON'T YOU GET IT?
THE ONE WHO HAS BEEN CREATING PORTALS TO THE ALTERNATE DIMENSION TO PROVIDE GUZMA WITH ULTRA BEASTS...
...THE ONE WHO IS PUTTING ALL OF ALOLA IN PERIL...

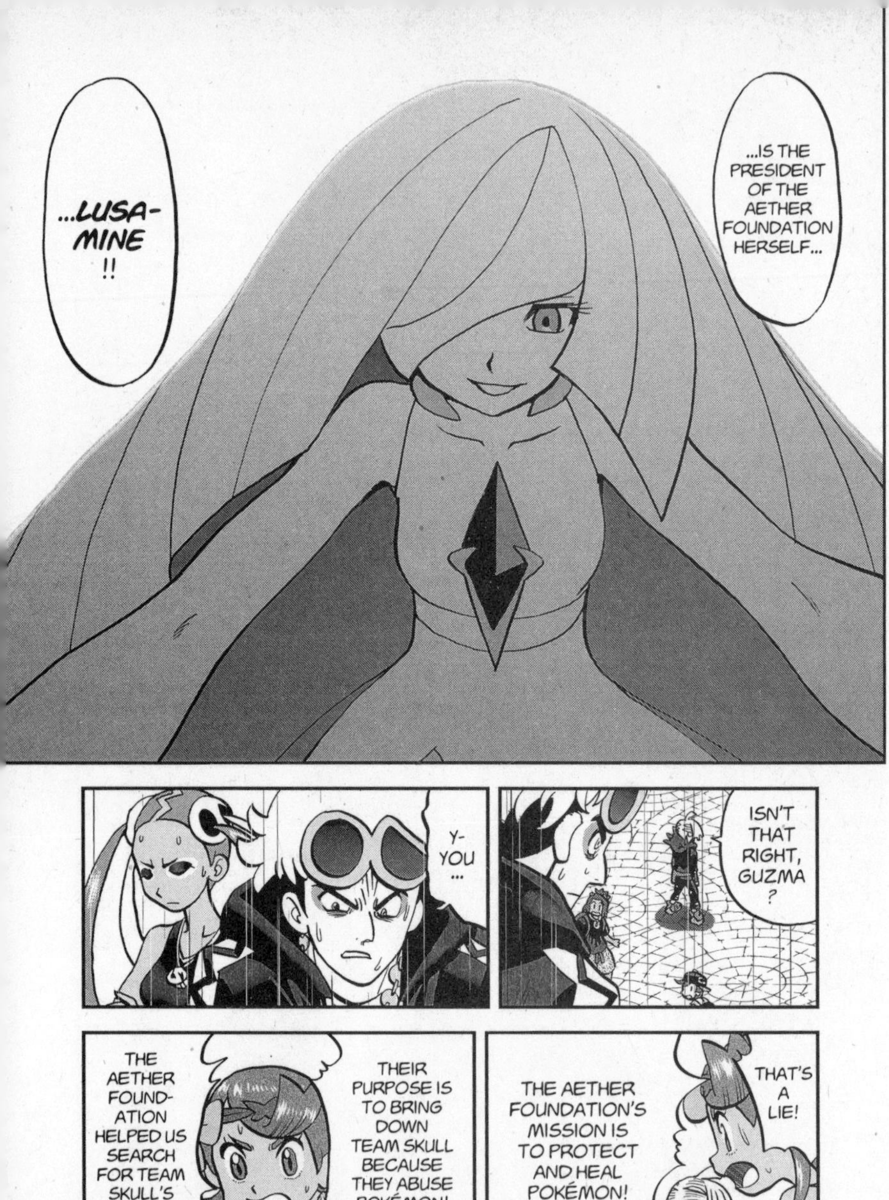
...IS THE PRESIDENT OF THE AETHER FOUNDATION HERSELF...
...LUSA-MINE !!
ISN'T THAT RIGHT, GUZMA?
Y-YOU ...
THAT'S A LIE!
THE AETHER FOUNDATION'S MISSION IS TO PROTECT AND HEAL POKÉMON!
THEIR PURPOSE IS TO BRING DOWN TEAM SKULL BECAUSE THEY ABUSE POKÉMON!
THE AETHER FOUND-ATION HELPED US SEARCH FOR TEAM SKULL'S HIDEOUT!

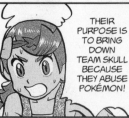

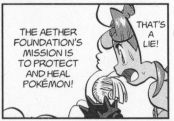

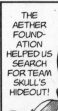

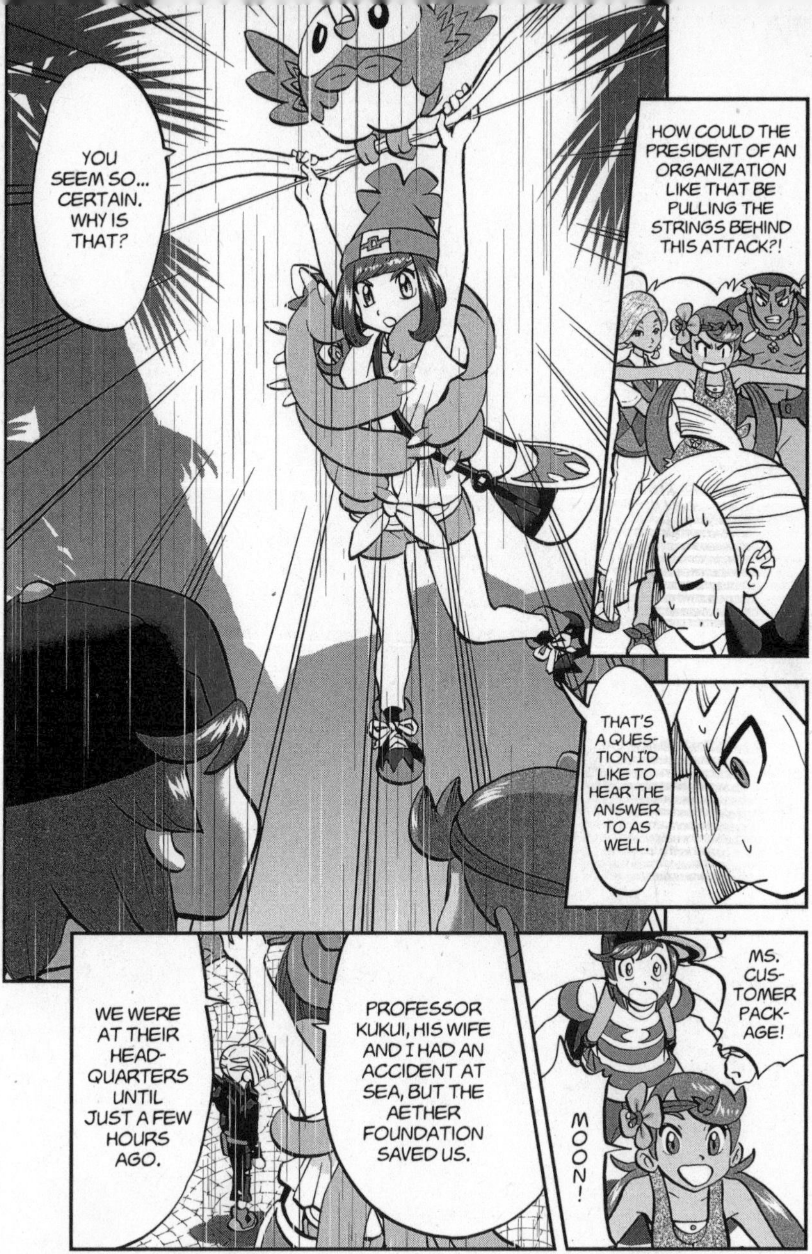
HOW COULD THE PRESIDENT OF AN ORGANIZATION LIKE THAT BE PULLING THE STRINGS BEHIND THIS ATTACK?!
THAT'S A QUESTION I'D LIKE TO HEAR THE ANSWER TO AS WELL.
YOU SEEM SO... CERTAIN. WHY IS THAT?
MS. CUSTOMER PACKAGE!
MOON!
PROFESSOR KUKUI, HIS WIFE AND I HAD AN ACCIDENT AT SEA, BUT THE AETHER FOUNDATION SAVED US.
WE WERE AT THEIR HEADQUARTERS UNTIL JUST A FEW HOURS AGO.

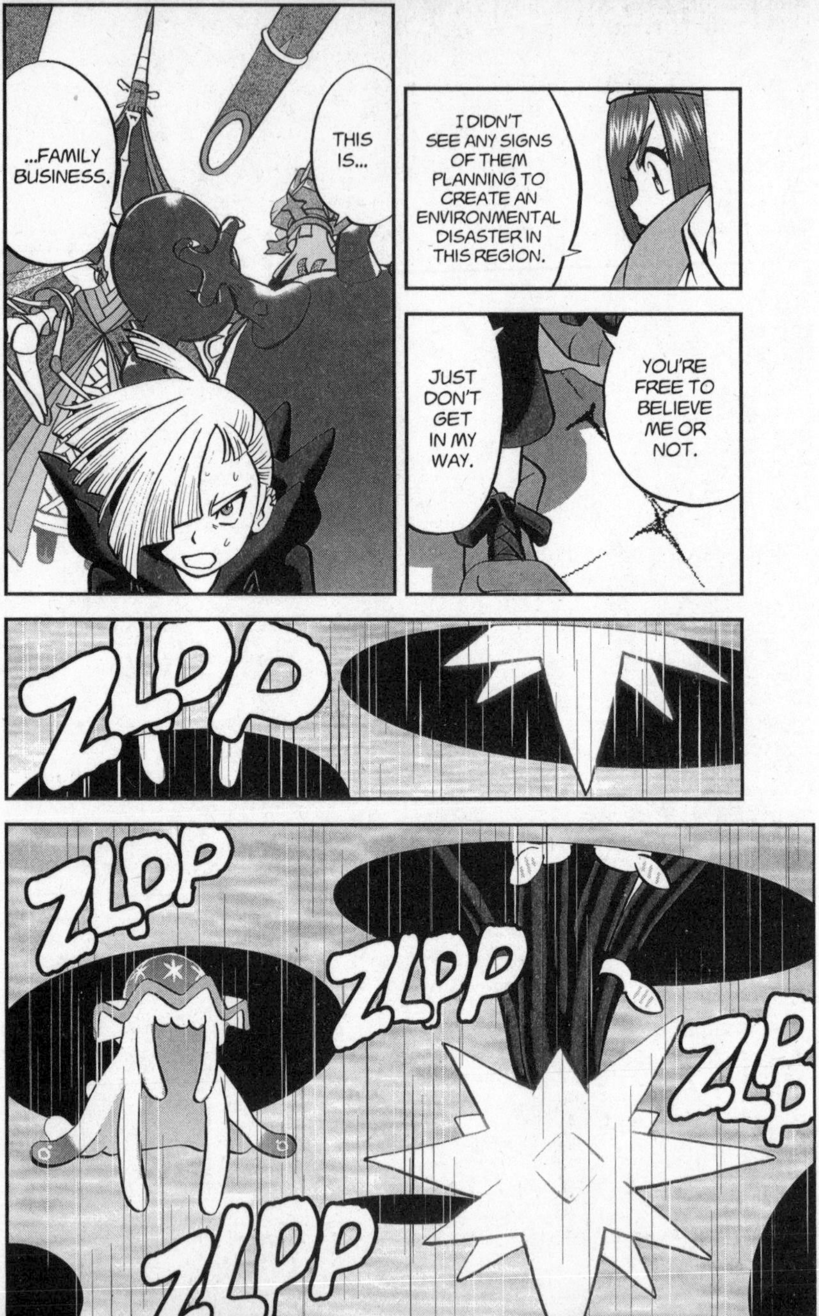
I DIDN'T SEE ANY SIGNS OF THEM PLANNING TO CREATE AN ENVIRONMENTAL DISASTER IN THIS REGION.
YOU'RE FREE TO BELIEVE ME OR NOT.
JUST DON'T GET IN MY WAY.
THIS IS...
...FAMILY BUSINESS.
ZLDP
ZLDP
ZLDP
ZLDP
ZLDP

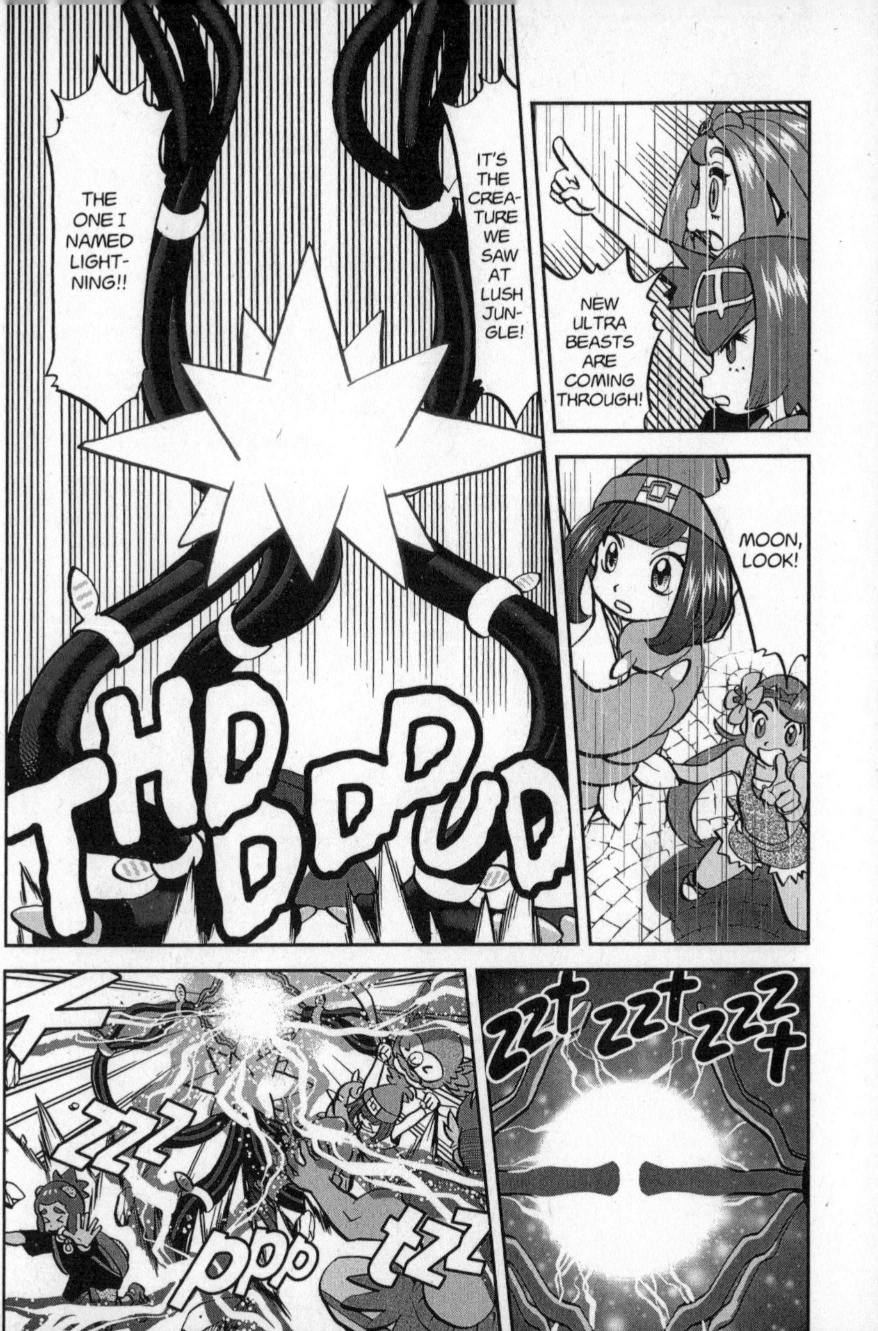
NEW ULTRA BEASTS ARE COMING THROUGH!
MOON, LOOK!
IT'S THE CREATURE WE SAW AT LUSH JUNGLE!
THE ONE I NAMED LIGHTNING!!
THDDDDUD
zzt zzt zzzt
zzz
ppp
tzz

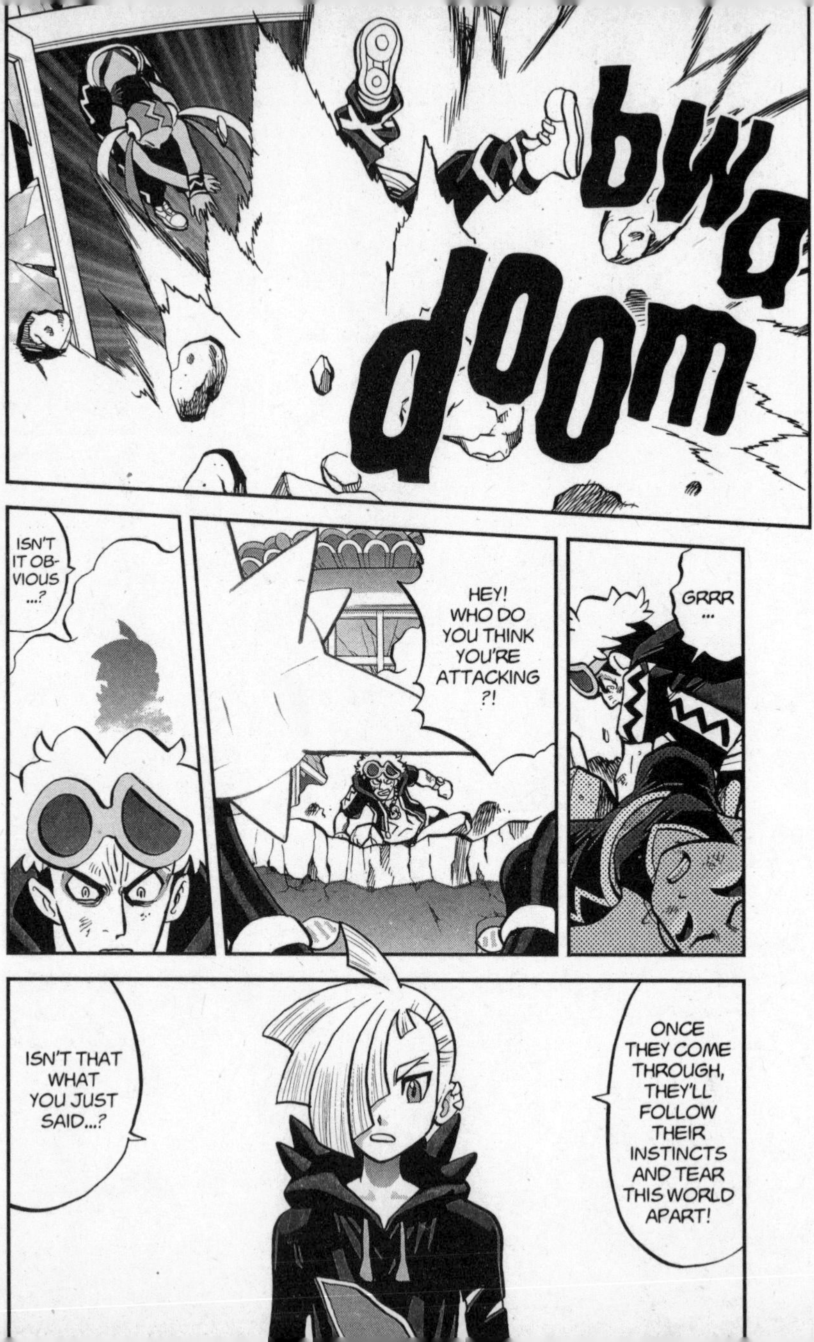
bwa doom
GRRR ...
HEY! WHO DO YOU THINK YOU'RE ATTACKING ?!
ISN'T IT OB-VIOUS ...?
ONCE THEY COME THROUGH, THEY'LL FOLLOW THEIR INSTINCTS AND TEAR THIS WORLD APART!
ISN'T THAT WHAT YOU JUST SAID...?

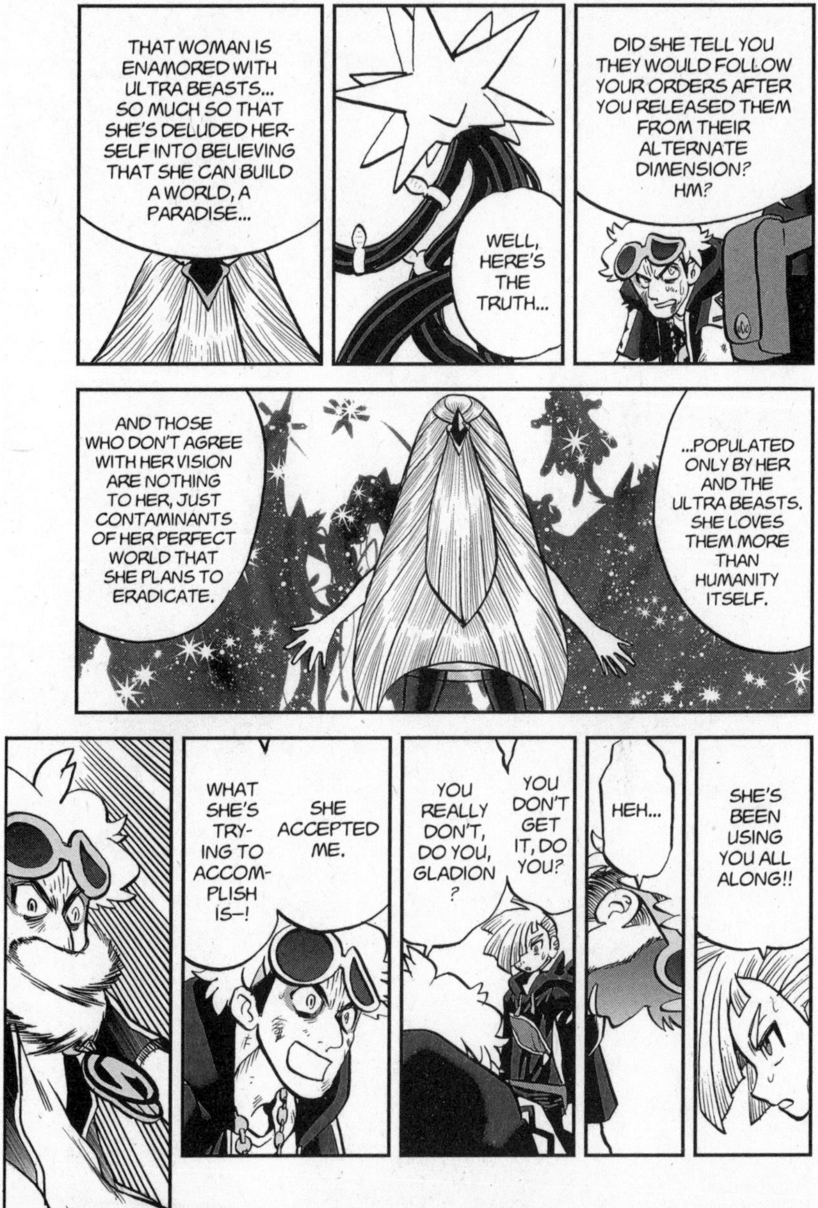
DID SHE TELL YOU THEY WOULD FOLLOW YOUR ORDERS AFTER YOU RELEASED THEM FROM THEIR ALTERNATE DIMENSION? HM?
WELL, HERE'S THE TRUTH...
THAT WOMAN IS ENAMORED WITH ULTRA BEASTS... SO MUCH SO THAT SHE'S DELUDED HER-SELF INTO BELIEVING THAT SHE CAN BUILD A WORLD, A PARADISE...
...POPULATED ONLY BY HER AND THE ULTRA BEASTS. SHE LOVES THEM MORE THAN HUMANITY ITSELF.
AND THOSE WHO DON'T AGREE WITH HER VISION ARE NOTHING TO HER, JUST CONTAMINANTS OF HER PERFECT WORLD THAT SHE PLANS TO ERADICATE.
SHE'S BEEN USING YOU ALL ALONG!!
HEH...
YOU DON'T GET IT, DO YOU?
YOU REALLY DON'T, DO YOU, GLADION?
SHE ACCEPTED ME.
WHAT SHE'S TRY-ING TO ACCOM-PLISH IS—!

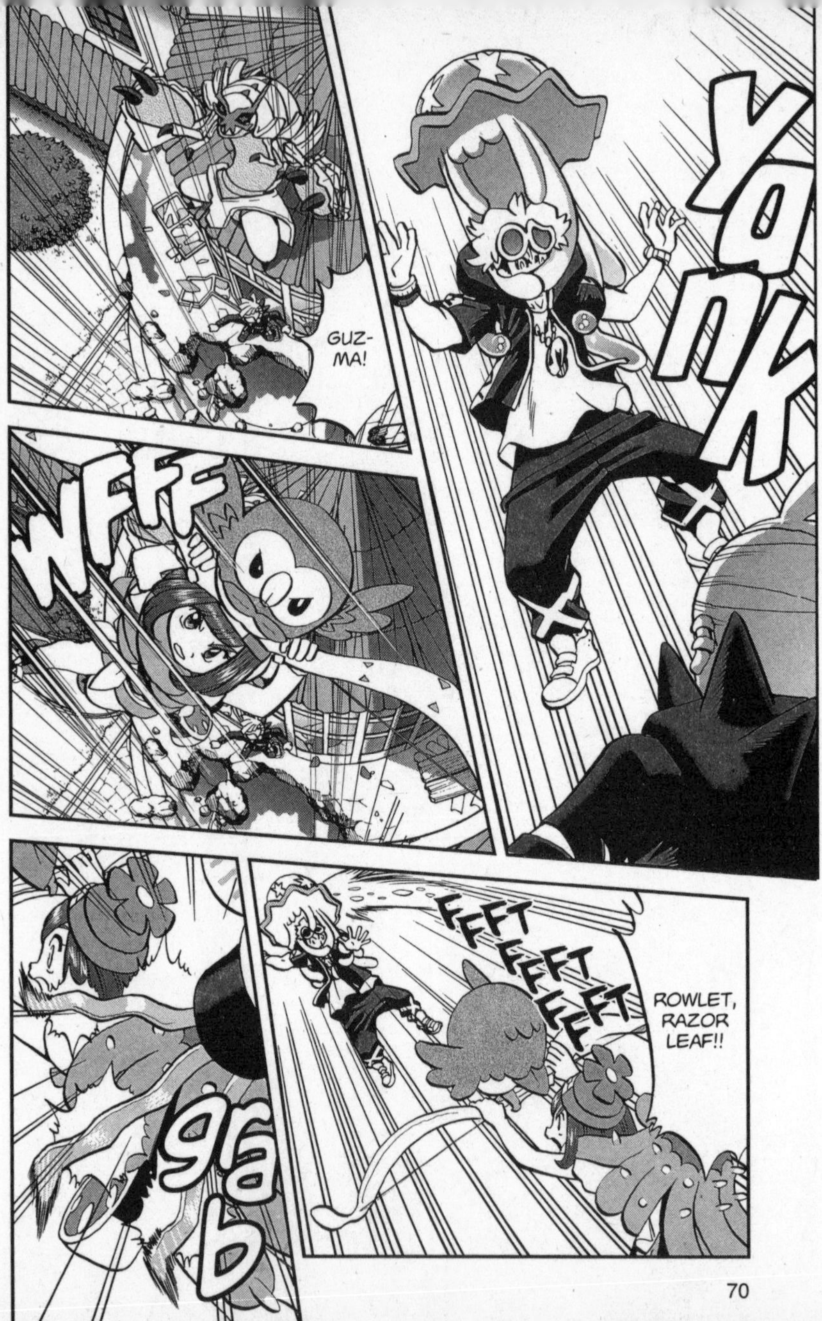
YANK
GUZ-MA!
WFFF
FFFT FFFT FFFT
ROWLET, RAZOR LEAF!!
grab

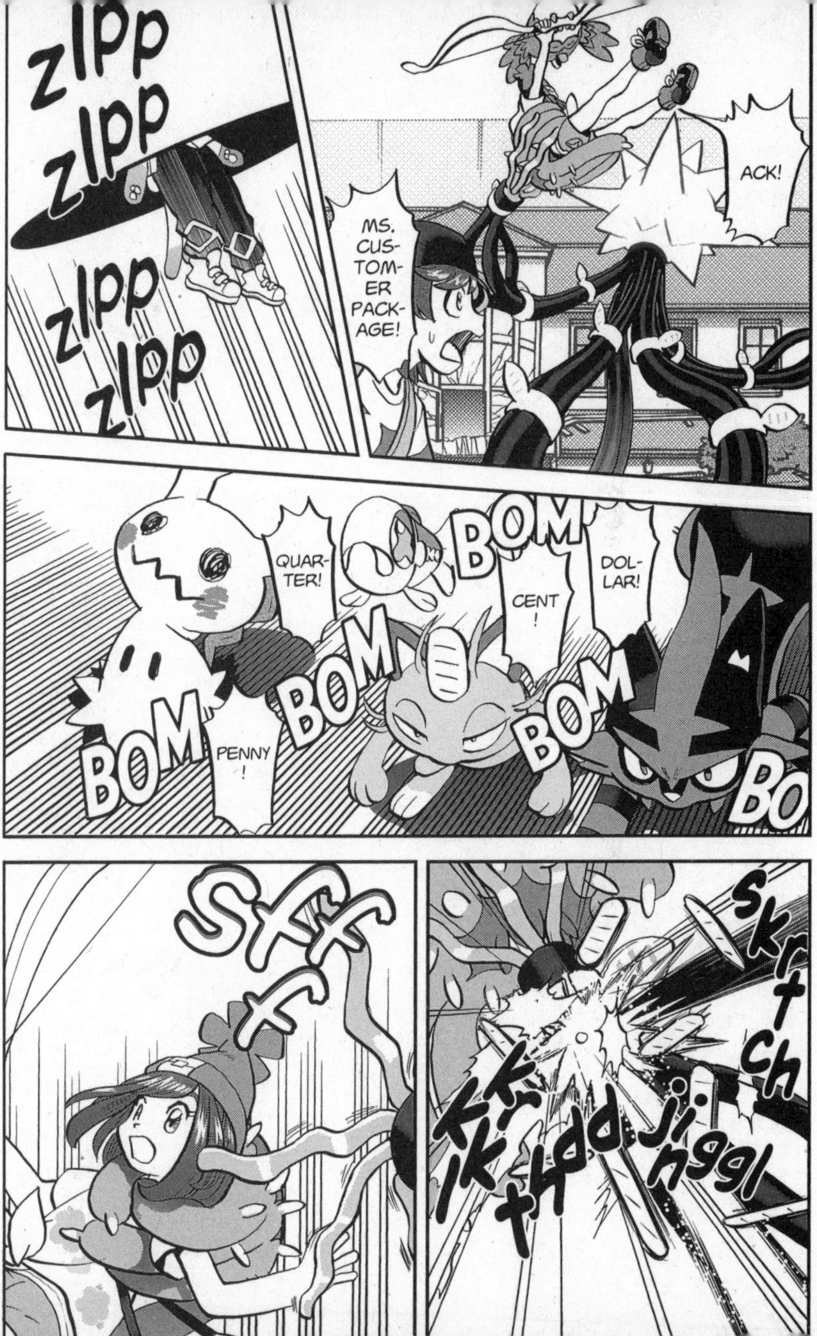
ACK!
MS. CUS-TOM-ER PACK-AGE!
zIPP zIPP zIPP
zIPP zIPP zIPP
BOM
DOL-LAR!
CENT!
QUAR-TER!
BOM
BOM
BOM
PENNY!
BOM
BO
skrrtch
jiggl
thdd
krik
Sfff

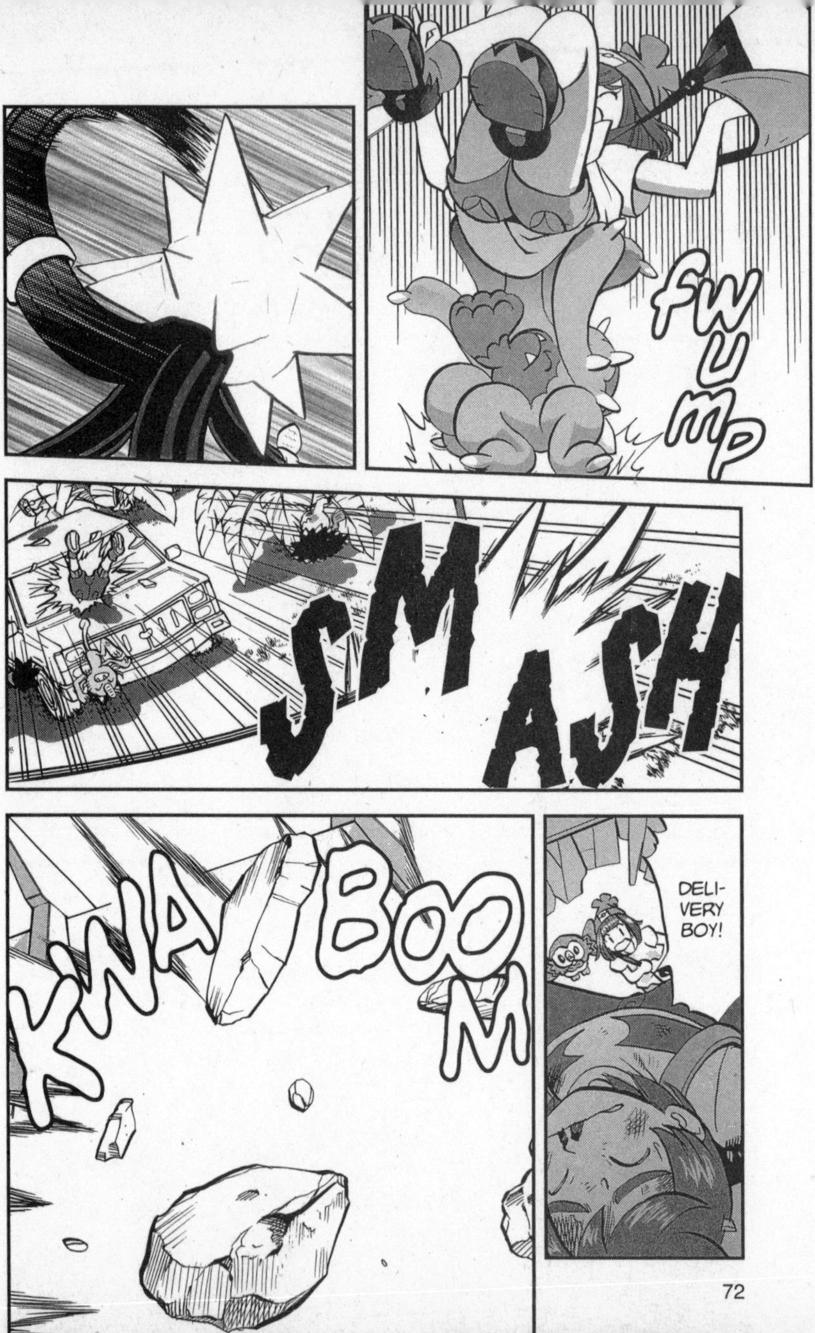
FWUMP
SMASH
DELI-VERY BOY!
K'WA BOOM

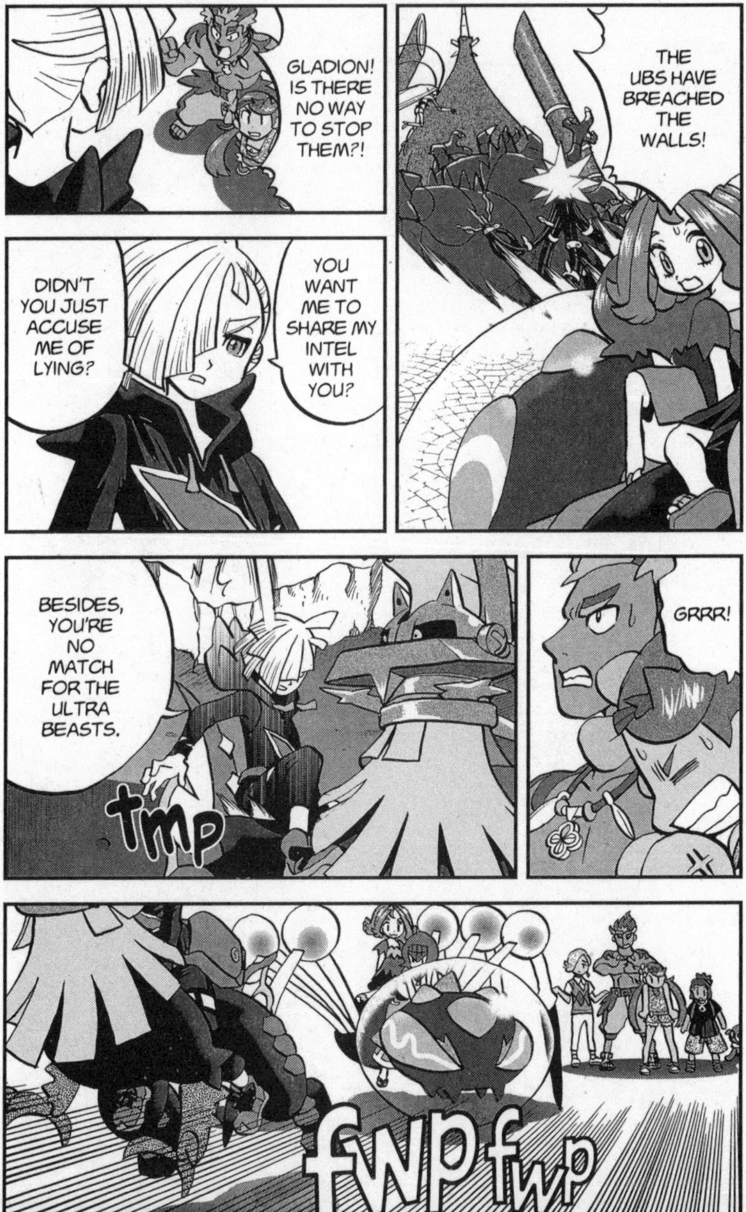
THE UBS HAVE BREACHED THE WALLS!
GLADION! IS THERE NO WAY TO STOP THEM?!
YOU WANT ME TO SHARE MY INTEL WITH YOU?
DIDN'T YOU JUST ACCUSE ME OF LYING?
GRRR!
BESIDES, YOU'RE NO MATCH FOR THE ULTRA BEASTS.
tmp
fwp fwp

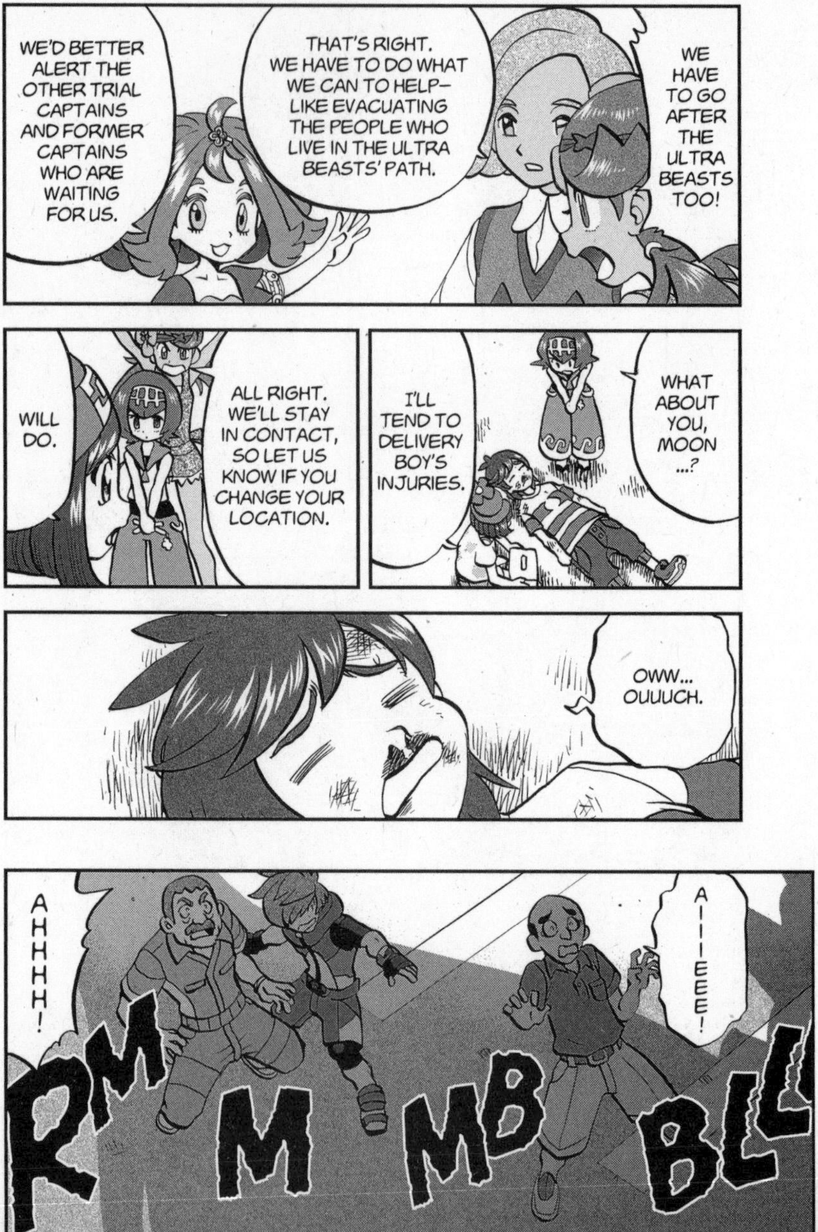
WE HAVE TO GO AFTER THE ULTRA BEASTS TOO!
THAT'S RIGHT. WE HAVE TO DO WHAT WE CAN TO HELP— LIKE EVACUATING THE PEOPLE WHO LIVE IN THE ULTRA BEASTS' PATH.
WE'D BETTER ALERT THE OTHER TRIAL CAPTAINS AND FORMER CAPTAINS WHO ARE WAITING FOR US.
WHAT ABOUT YOU, MOON ...?
I'LL TEND TO DELIVERY BOY'S INJURIES.
ALL RIGHT. WE'LL STAY IN CONTACT, SO LET US KNOW IF YOU CHANGE YOUR LOCATION.
WILL DO.
OWW... OUUUCH.
AIIEEE!
AHHHH!
RM M MB BLL

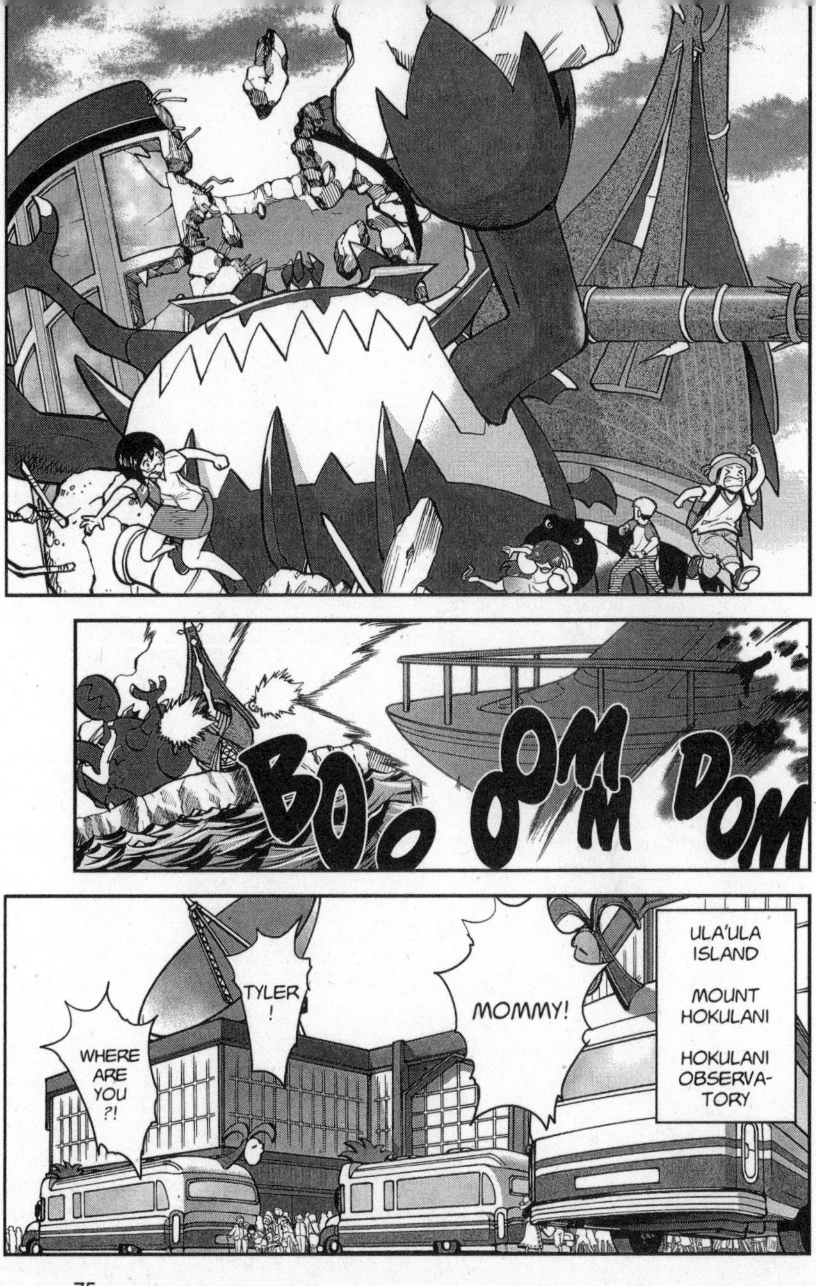
BOOOM DOM DOM
ULA'ULA ISLAND
MOUNT HOKULANI
HOKULANI OBSERVATORY
MOMMY!
TYLER!
WHERE ARE YOU?!

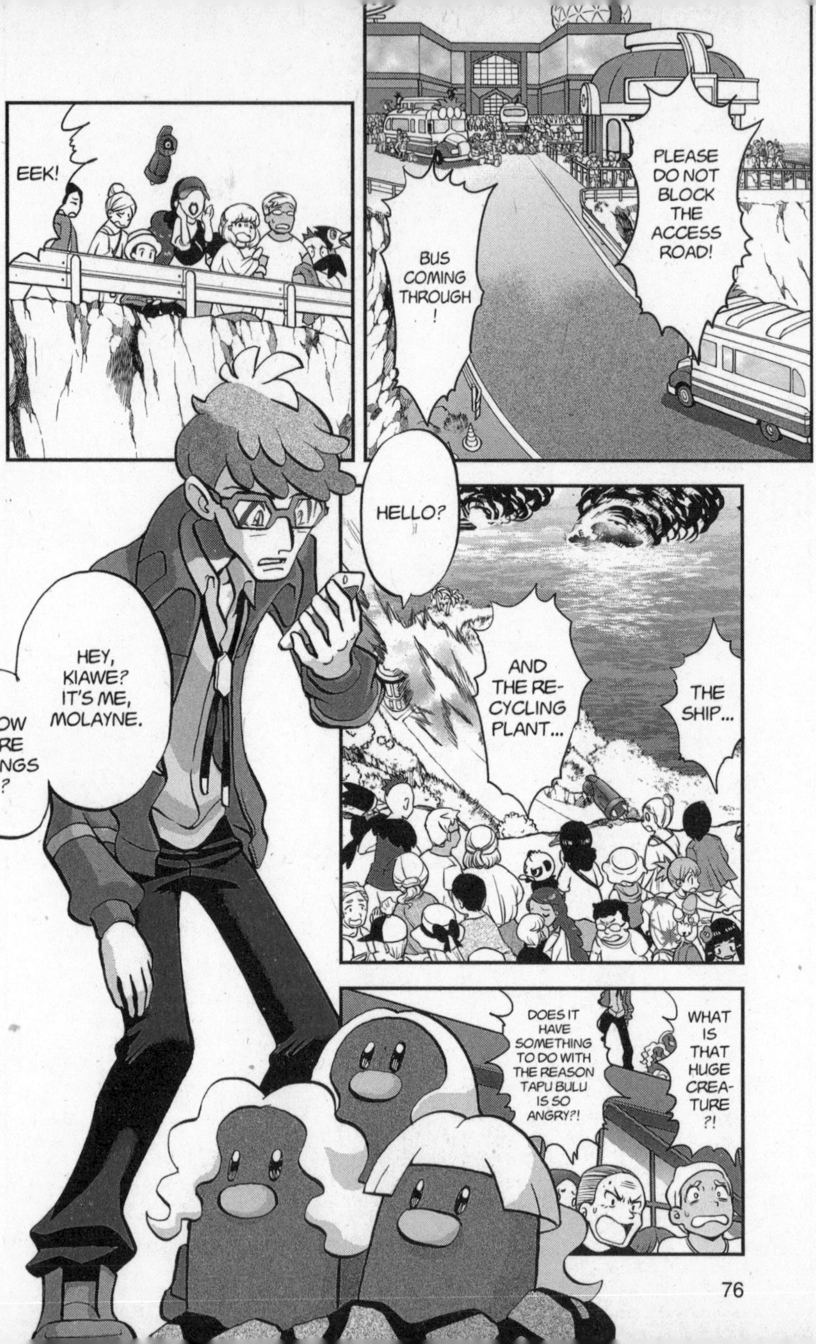
PLEASE DO NOT BLOCK THE ACCESS ROAD!
BUS COMING THROUGH!
EEK!
THE SHIP...
AND THE RE-CYCLING PLANT...
WHAT IS THAT HUGE CREA-TURE?!
DOES IT HAVE SOMETHING TO DO WITH THE REASON TAPU BULU IS SO ANGRY?!
HELLO?
HEY, KIAWE? IT'S ME, MOLAYNE.
HOW ARE THINGS?

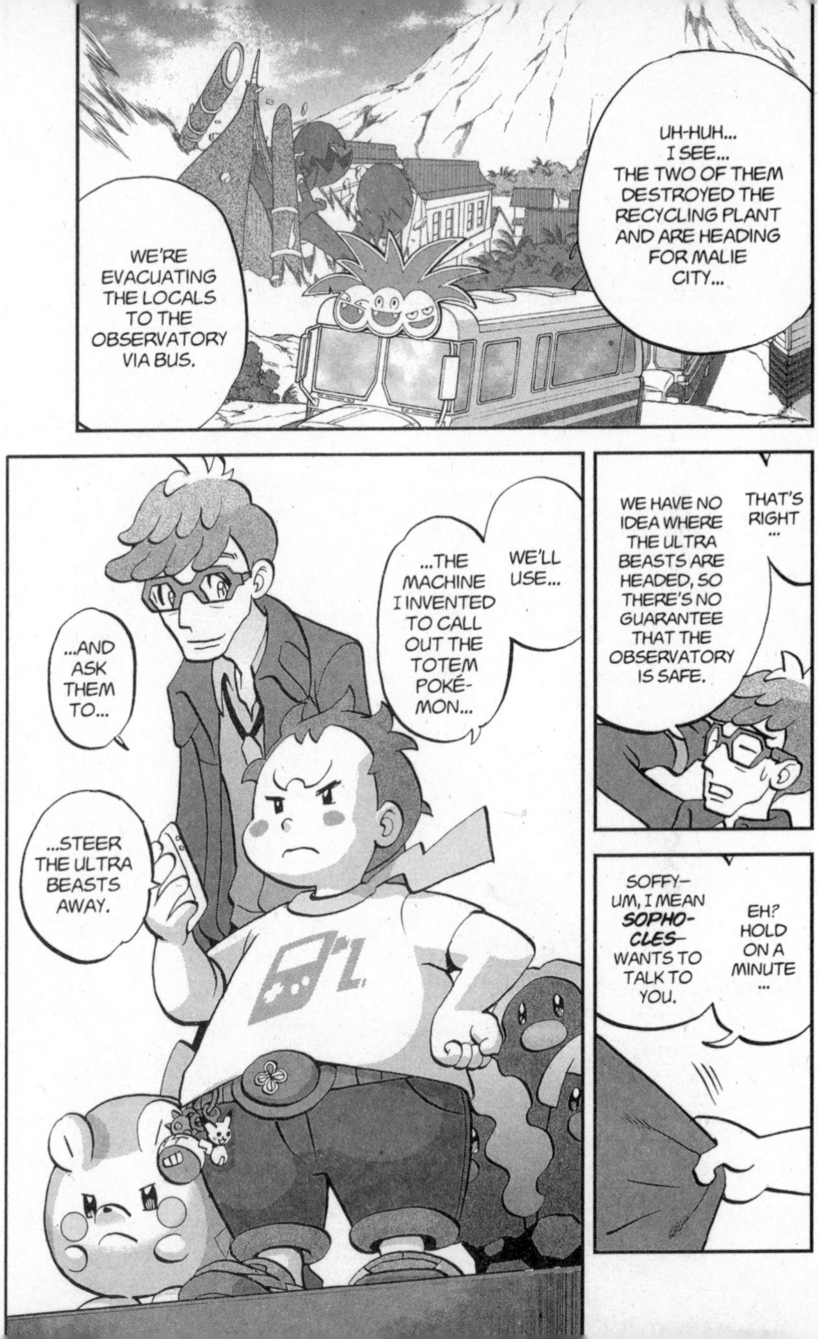
UH-HUH... I SEE... THE TWO OF THEM DESTROYED THE RECYCLING PLANT AND ARE HEADING FOR MALIE CITY...
WE'RE EVACUATING THE LOCALS TO THE OBSERVATORY VIA BUS.
THAT'S RIGHT...
WE HAVE NO IDEA WHERE THE ULTRA BEASTS ARE HEADED, SO THERE'S NO GUARANTEE THAT THE OBSERVATORY IS SAFE.
EH? HOLD ON A MINUTE...
SOFFY— UM, I MEAN **SOPHOCLES**— WANTS TO TALK TO YOU.
WE'LL USE...
...THE MACHINE I INVENTED TO CALL OUT THE TOTEM POKÉMON...
...AND ASK THEM TO...
...STEER THE ULTRA BEASTS AWAY.

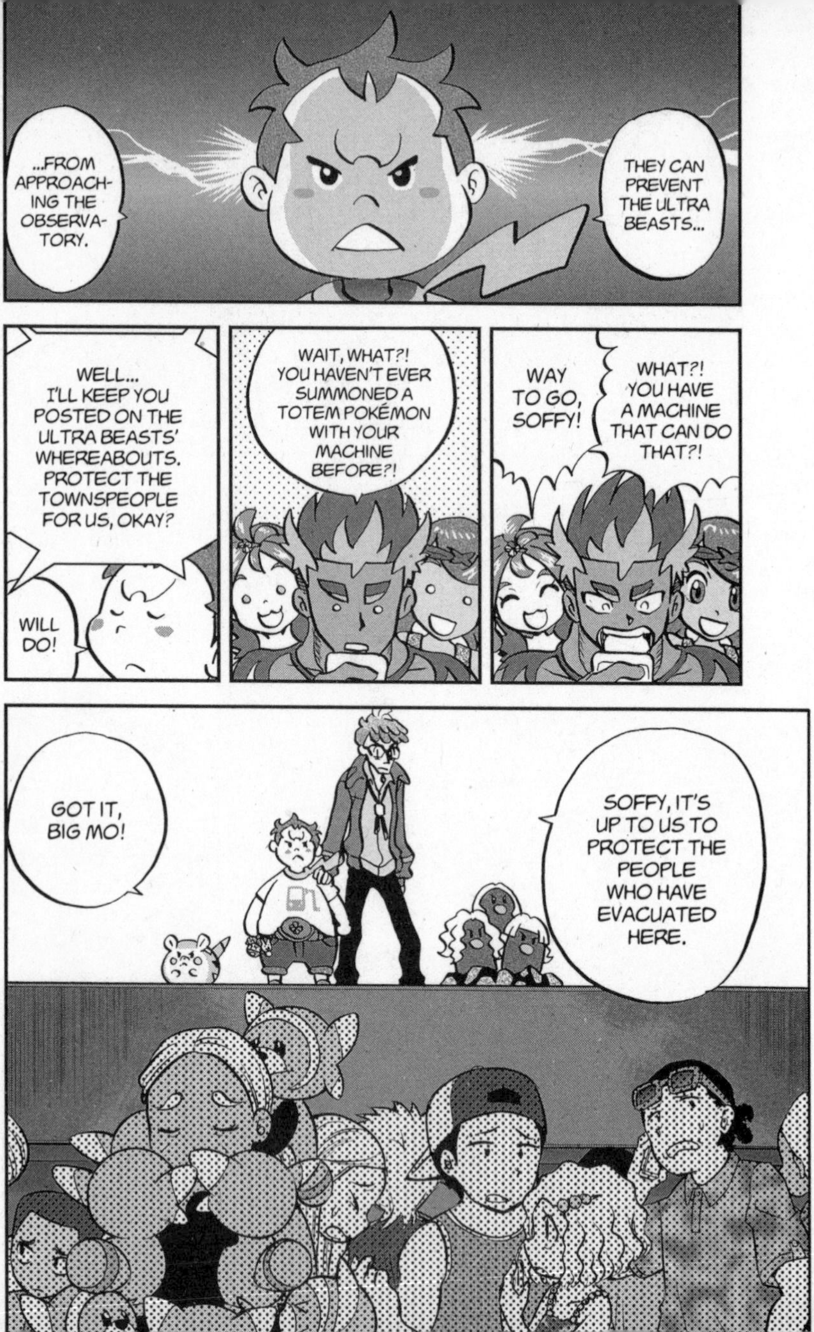
THEY CAN PREVENT THE ULTRA BEASTS...
...FROM APPROACHING THE OBSERVATORY.
WHAT?! YOU HAVE A MACHINE THAT CAN DO THAT?!
WAY TO GO, SOFFY!
WAIT, WHAT?! YOU HAVEN'T EVER SUMMONED A TOTEM POKÉMON WITH YOUR MACHINE BEFORE?!
WELL... I'LL KEEP YOU POSTED ON THE ULTRA BEASTS' WHEREABOUTS. PROTECT THE TOWNSPEOPLE FOR US, OKAY?
WILL DO!
SOFFY, IT'S UP TO US TO PROTECT THE PEOPLE WHO HAVE EVACUATED HERE.
GOT IT, BIG MO!

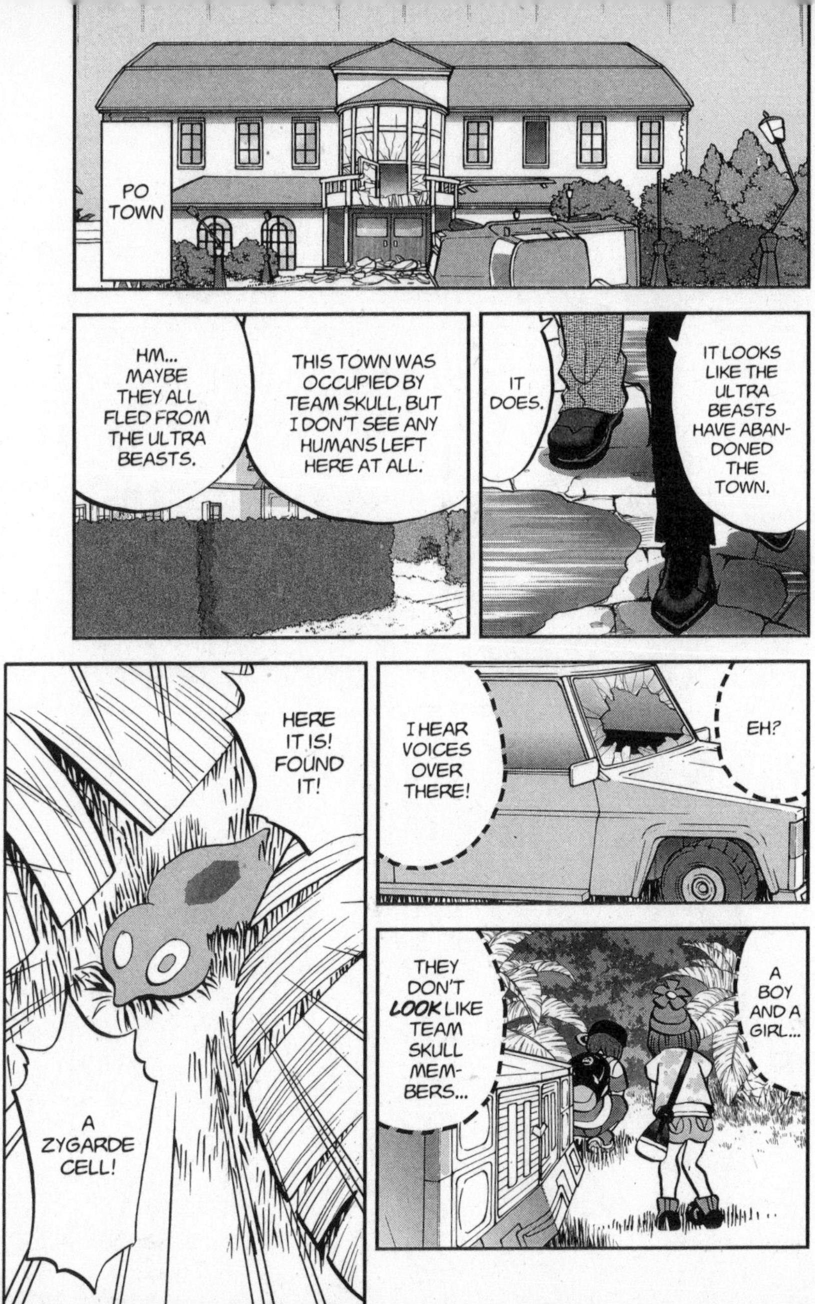
PO TOWN
IT LOOKS LIKE THE ULTRA BEASTS HAVE ABAN-DONED THE TOWN.
IT DOES.
THIS TOWN WAS OCCUPIED BY TEAM SKULL, BUT I DON'T SEE ANY HUMANS LEFT HERE AT ALL.
HM... MAYBE THEY ALL FLED FROM THE ULTRA BEASTS.
EH?
I HEAR VOICES OVER THERE!
A BOY AND A GIRL...
THEY DON'T **LOOK** LIKE TEAM SKULL MEM-BERS...
HERE IT IS! FOUND IT!
A ZYGARDE CELL!

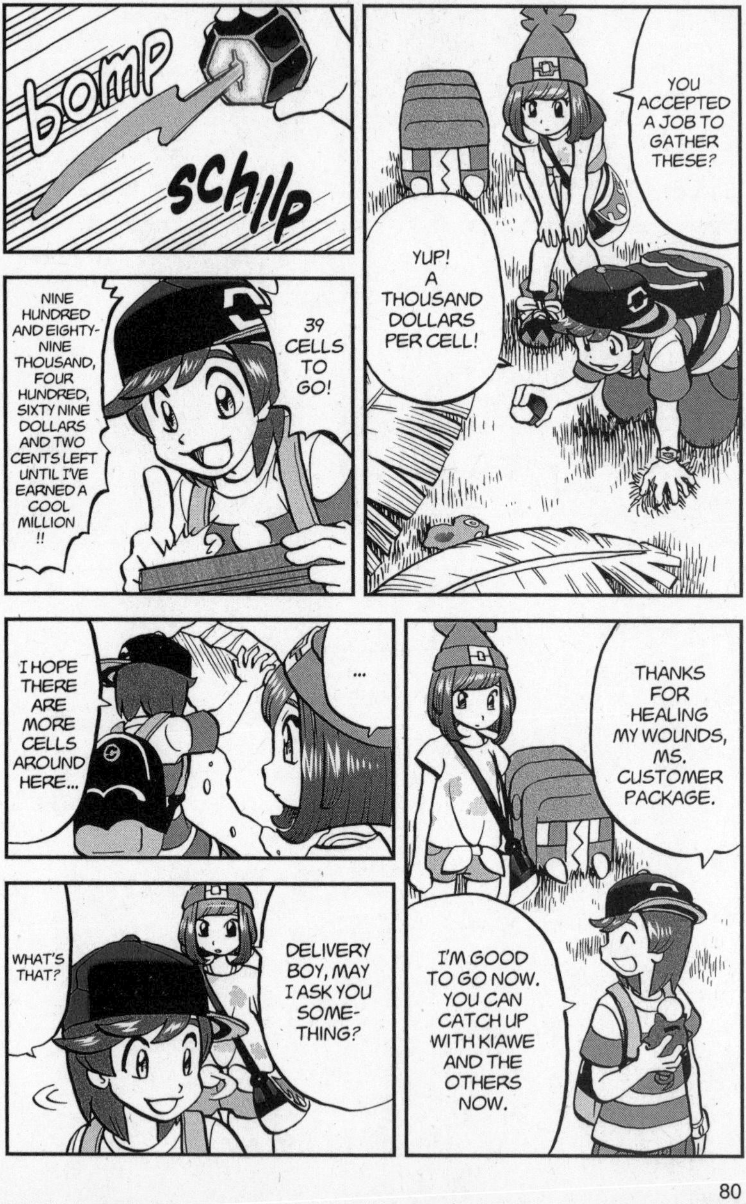
YOU ACCEPTED A JOB TO GATHER THESE?
YUP! A THOUSAND DOLLARS PER CELL!
bomp
schlip
39 CELLS TO GO!
NINE HUNDRED AND EIGHTY-NINE THOUSAND, FOUR HUNDRED, SIXTY NINE DOLLARS AND TWO CENTS LEFT UNTIL I'VE EARNED A COOL MILLION !!
THANKS FOR HEALING MY WOUNDS, MS. CUSTOMER PACKAGE.
I'M GOOD TO GO NOW. YOU CAN CATCH UP WITH KIAWE AND THE OTHERS NOW.
...
I HOPE THERE ARE MORE CELLS AROUND HERE...
DELIVERY BOY, MAY I ASK YOU SOME-THING?
WHAT'S THAT?

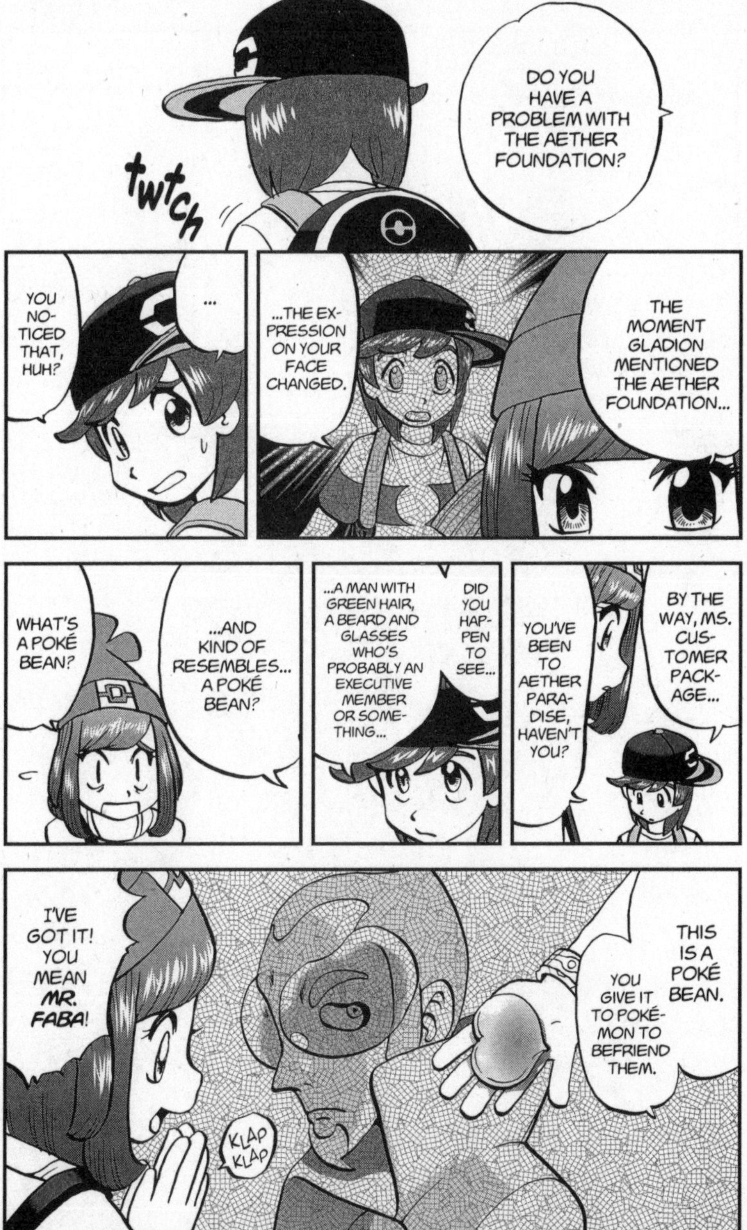
DO YOU HAVE A PROBLEM WITH THE AETHER FOUNDATION?
twtch
THE MOMENT GLADION MENTIONED THE AETHER FOUNDATION...
...THE EXPRESSION ON YOUR FACE CHANGED.
...
YOU NOTICED THAT, HUH?
BY THE WAY, MS. CUSTOMER PACKAGE...
YOU'VE BEEN TO AETHER PARADISE, HAVEN'T YOU?
DID YOU HAPPEN TO SEE...
...A MAN WITH GREEN HAIR, A BEARD AND GLASSES WHO'S PROBABLY AN EXECUTIVE MEMBER OR SOMETHING...
...AND KIND OF RESEMBLES... A POKÉ BEAN?
WHAT'S A POKÉ BEAN?
THIS IS A POKÉ BEAN.
YOU GIVE IT TO POKÉMON TO BEFRIEND THEM.
I'VE GOT IT! YOU MEAN *MR. FABA*!
KLAP KLAP

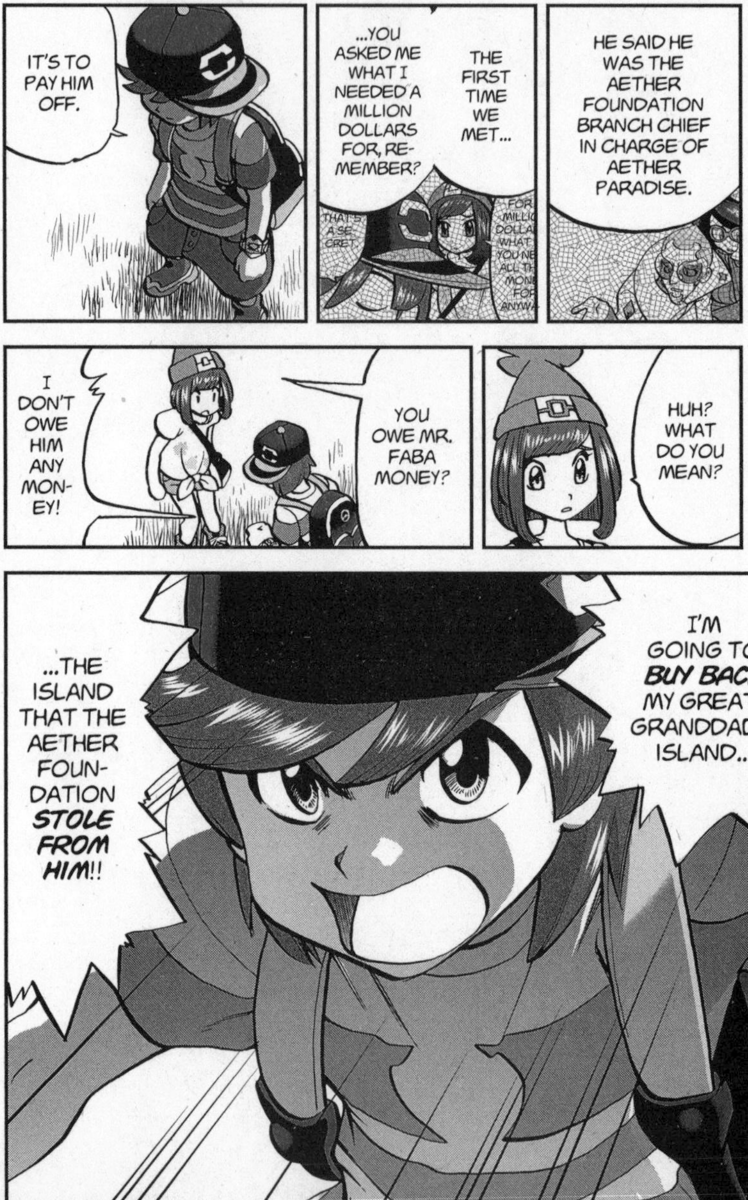
HE SAID HE WAS THE AETHER FOUNDATION BRANCH CHIEF IN CHARGE OF AETHER PARADISE.
THE FIRST TIME WE MET...
...YOU ASKED ME WHAT I NEEDED A MILLION DOLLARS FOR, RE-MEMBER?
THAT'S A SE-CRET
IT'S TO PAY HIM OFF.
HUH? WHAT DO YOU MEAN?
YOU OWE MR. FABA MONEY?
I DON'T OWE HIM ANY MON-EY!
I'M GOING TO **BUY BACK** MY GREAT-GRANDDAD'S ISLAND...
...THE ISLAND THAT THE AETHER FOUN-DATION **STOLE FROM HIM**!!

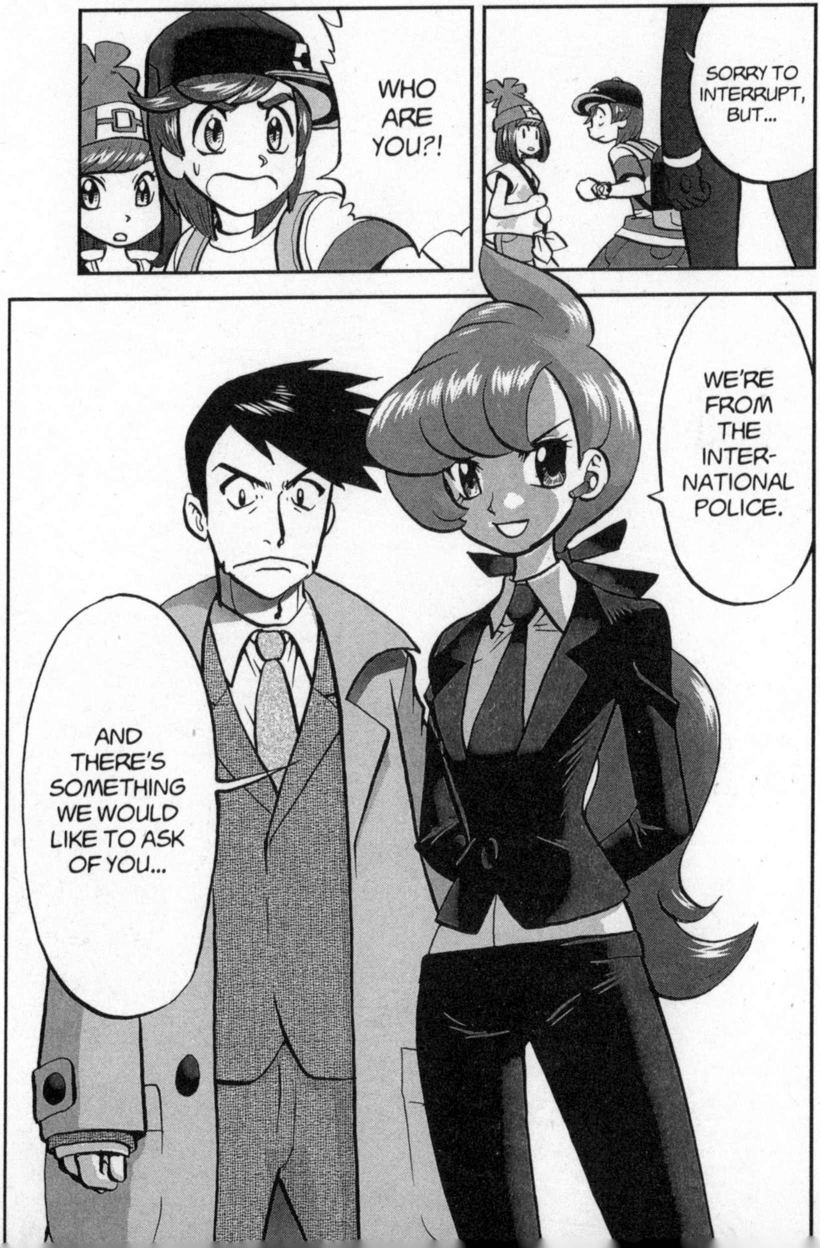
SORRY TO INTERRUPT, BUT...
WHO ARE YOU?!
WE'RE FROM THE INTER-NATIONAL POLICE.
AND THERE'S SOMETHING WE WOULD LIKE TO ASK OF YOU...

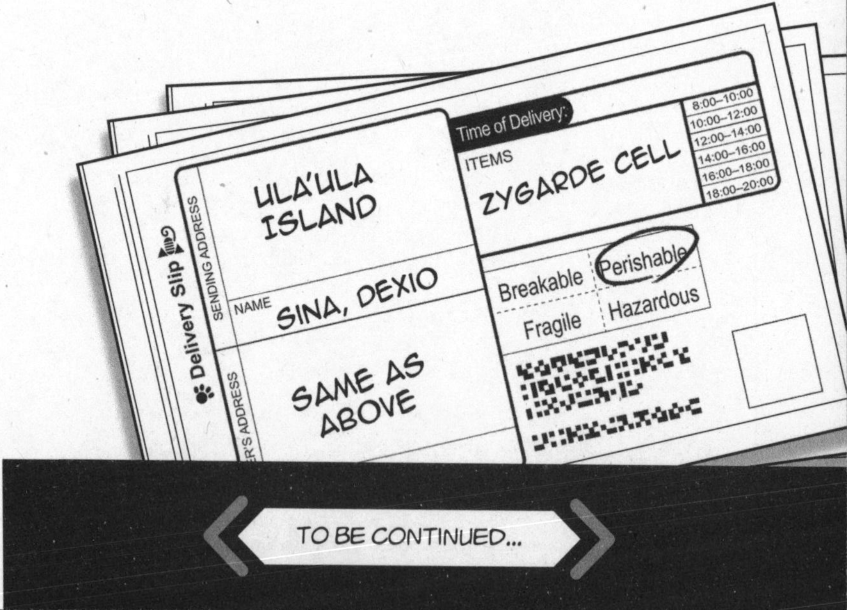
Delivery Slip
SENDING ADDRESS
ULA'ULA ISLAND
NAME
SINA, DEXIO
SAME AS ABOVE
Time of Delivery:
ITEMS
ZYGARDE CELL
8:00–10:00
10:00–12:00
12:00–14:00
14:00–16:00
16:00–18:00
18:00–20:00
Breakable
Perishable
Fragile
Hazardous
TO BE CONTINUED...

Pokémon Sun & Moon
Volume 6
VIZ Media Edition

Story by HIDENORI KUSAKA
Art by SATOSHI YAMAMOTO

©2020 The Pokémon Company International.
©1995–2018 Nintendo / Creatures Inc. / GAME FREAK inc.
TM, ®, and character names are trademarks of Nintendo.
POCKET MONSTERS SPECIAL SUN • MOON Vol. 3
by Hidenori KUSAKA, Satoshi YAMAMOTO
© 2017 Hidenori KUSAKA, Satoshi YAMAMOTO
All rights reserved.
Original Japanese edition published by SHOGAKUKAN.
English translation rights in the United States of America, Canada, the United Kingdom,
Ireland, Australia and New Zealand arranged with SHOGAKUKAN.

Original Cover Design—Hiroyuki KAWASOME (grafio)

English Adaptation—Bryant Turnage
Translation—Tetsuichiro Miyaki
Touch-Up & Lettering—Susan Daigle-Leach
Design—Alice Lewis
Editor—Annette Roman

The stories, characters and incidents mentioned
in this publication are entirely fictional.

No portion of this book may be reproduced or transmitted
in any form or by any means without written permission
from the copyright holders.

Printed in the U.S.A.

Published by
VIZ Media, LLC
P.O. Box 77010
San Francisco, CA 94107

10 9 8 7 6 5 4 3 2 1
First printing, January 2020

PARENTAL ADVISORY
POKÉMON ADVENTURES is rated A
and is suitable for readers of all ages.

viz.com

Coming Next Volume

Volume 7

International Police officers Looker and Anabel arrive on the scene and hire Sun to help them pursue the mysterious Ultra Beasts—and not a moment too soon, because the Ultra Beasts are attacking one island after another in the Alola region! And then, a group of Crabrawler steals Sun's special berry!

What is the shocking secret of Anabel's origin?

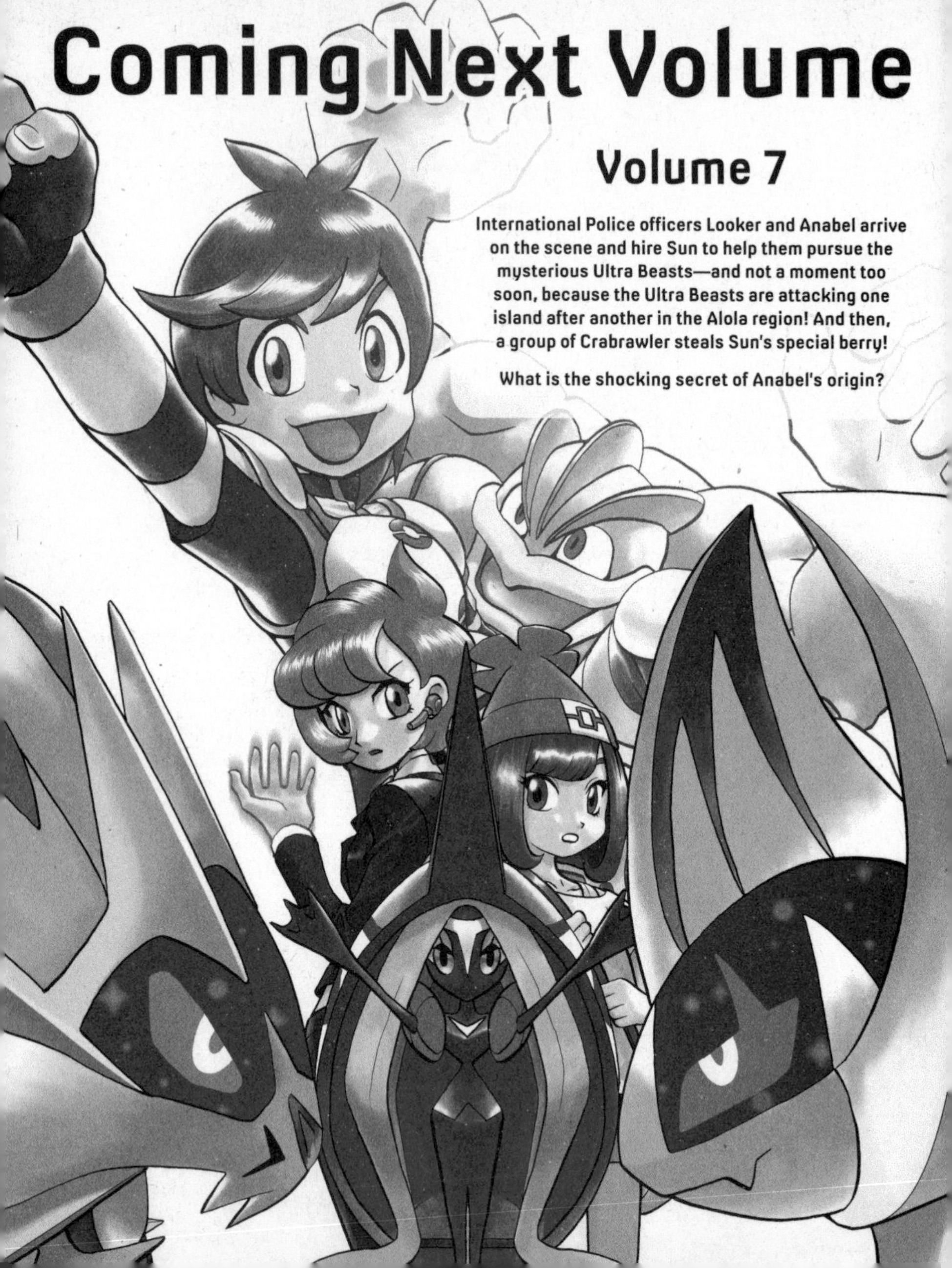

POKÉMON
SEEK AND FIND

Find your favorite Pokémon in five different full-color activity books! Pick your adventure: will you search for the special Pokémon of Kanto, Johto, or Hoenn? Or will you seek fan favorites like Pikachu or Legendary Pokémon? Each book includes tons of Pokémon-packed seek-and-find illustrations as well as fun facts or creative quizzes about the Pokémon inside.

©2018 The Pokémon Company International. ©1995-2015 Nintendo / Creatures Inc. / GAME FREAK inc. TM, ®, and character names are trademarks of Nintendo.

viz.com

Received On

FEB 0 9 2021

Magnolia

THIS IS THE END OF THIS GRAPHIC NOVEL!

To properly enjoy this VIZ Media graphic novel, please turn it around and begin reading from right to left.

This book has been printed in the original Japanese format in order to preserve the orientation of the original artwork. Have fun with it!

‹‹‹ READ THIS WAY!

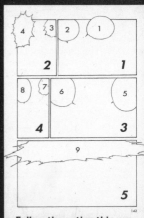

Follow the action this way.